Horace Deluscar

Merris

And other Poems

Horace Deluscar

Merris
And other Poems

ISBN/EAN: 9783337206406

Printed in Europe, USA, Canada, Australia, Japan

Cover: Foto ©Andreas Hilbeck / pixelio.de

More available books at **www.hansebooks.com**

DELUSCAR'S MERRIS

AND

OTHER POEMS

BY

HORACE DELUSCAR

GAY AND BIRD

22 BEDFORD STREET, STRAND

LONDON

1899

Edinburgh : T. and A. CONSTABLE, Printers to Her Majesty

A NEW YEAR'S WISH TO MERRIS

I wish thee a' thy soul's desire,
I wish thee a' thy heart's delight,
Nae broken strings in thy life's lyre,
Amang thy roses ne'er a blight,
Nor weeping ees nor darksome days,
But sunny, gentle, peacefu' rest,—
Of a' the world's lovely Mays,
For me thou 'rt ever far the best.

THOSE who think rhyme should always be exact
—a mere cling-clang of sweet-sounding octaves—
should study Burns's 'Castle o' Montgomery.'

The grandest music is ever that wherein the
discords are as frequent as in life itself; and,
as in life, the constant recurrence of exact
similarities becomes a wearisome nuisance.

The deep, full-mouthed words of the Eliza-
bethan days must not be looked for here,—
life is not now, as then, a tragedy.

Horace Deluscar is, for justifiable reasons,
an assumed name. The author is Glasgow
born, Berwickshire bred, and of Midlothian
and Fife extraction.

CONTENTS

CONTENTS

MISCELLANEOUS—

DELUSCAR'S MERRIS
AND OTHER POEMS

SONNET

As a tall, gloomy building blazons high
Upon his forehead one bright jewelled name,
Frowning in darkness as the letters die,
Through swift withdrawal of their jetting flame,
To smile again in rays of rosy light
The instant that the sweet name reappears,
So smile I when you cross my inward sight,
Who otherwise am gloomy unto tears ;
And latter-day dissectors of my style
Shall say, ' He thought of lovely Merris here ;
For as those lamps in beauty grace that pile,
Her influence makes his verse ring sweet and
        clear;
    Chaste as the moon upon her silver throne,
    She decks him in a glory not his own.'

THE COVENANTER

WHEN the day's upon the gloaming
  And the wind is in the West,
A' my thochts, they gang a-roaming
  On the lass that I lo'e best.
Is she sad like me, and weary,
  Weary a' the nicht sae laug,
Parted frae the only dearie
  In the mighty warld's thrang?

See, the moon's in marriage veiling,
  And the dainty choiring stars
A' in bridal silver sailing—
  Notes in heaven's music-bars!
While my love and I are parted
  Naething can us comfort gie;
And when baith are broken-hearted,
  What is left us but to dee?

Oh, the raptures of our meeting
  In the days of long ago,
When she couldna speak for greeting
  In her joy to haud me so!—

Clasped unto her modest bosom
  While my kisses fell like rain,
Sic a winsome lass and lo'esome
  Time shall never see again !

Cruel Fortune, be propitious !
  A' your tortures, a' your pain,
I wad bear 't and ca 'd delicious
  If ye 'll gie me her, my ain.
In the yonder, past the gloaming,
  Where the days are ever fair,
Past this weary, weary homing,
  We shall meet to part nae mair.

THE COVENANTER'S LASSIE

And will he no' come back again,
　　That's a' the world to me,
And maun I daunder here my lane,
　　The saut tears in my e'e?

I've made his hame as bright as bright
　　Now Clavers' deid and gane,
And Scotland's sword has set her right
　　And gotten back her ain.

I've wrocht my fingers near the bane,
　　I'd do it a' and mair,
To gather what was yince his ain
　　And start him fresh and fair.

There's nowte and sheep intil the fauld,
　　There's kye intil the byre,
His faither and his mither auld
　　Are cuddling ower the fire.

His guid grey mare, his collie dog,
    I 'll neither gie nor len',
For baith the twa were at Drumclog
    And suffered sairly then.

To meet them made my heart fu' sair,
    Masterless hirpling hame,
The dog aye cheering on the mare,
    Baith gashed and tired, but game.

Tho' I mysel' should gang withoot
    And beg frae toon to toon,
They shall be fed, each gallant brute,
    Wi' measures heaped aboon !

It canna be, my gallant lad
    That stormed the ranks of war,
That a' their prisons couldna haud
    That reached the Hollands far.

It canna be but he 'll win hame,
    My lad that waured them a' ;
I tell the neebors, ' Fie, for shame !
    To hae their doots ava.'

When hope is low to eerie lowe
    And faith begins to reist,
He 'll stagger weary up the knowe
    Unto this faithfu' breist !

For God is guid, and Scots are dour
    To grip the biggest odds ;
And aye that kind, ye may be sure,
    Are favourites of God's.

THE COVENANTER'S RETURN

'Hame!' dearest word in a' the world—
Except anither, 'free,'
And 'love,' that's far and far away
The sweetest o' the three.

'And it's hame, hame, hame,
Fain wad I be hame
To my ain countree.'

And I am free—at last at hame
Wi' thee, my bonnie dearie,
My ain folk—neebours—a' the same,
And a'thing bright and cheery.

My very collie, barking, snowks
And rives my bannet frae me,
And twenty dizzen holes he howks
Wi' perfect joy to see me.

The bonnic burn that wimples by
    The gowans through the clachan,
The sea, the hills, the sweeping sky,
    The moors wi' heather laughin'.

The Bens conversing wi' the stars
    In their eternal sentry,
The screams of eagles up the scaurs,
    Of whaups in laigher country.

I feel 't, I hear 't, I canna see 't,
    My een are sooming rarely—
What can a strong man do but greet
    Like me, and break down sairly ?

Frae foreign dreams o' thee and them
    To waken was Gehenna,
To find me free wi' thee at hame,
    Thank God eneuch I canna.

And as for thee, the fairest, best
    That e'er to man was given,
Clasping me to thy faithfu' breast,
    What is 't but perfect heaven ?

To comfort thee, my bonnie doo,
Wi' day's darg, late and early,
I 'll make the sickle, spade, and ploo
Fill up the measure fairly.

In praise to God that joined us here
Ring high our native valley,
They needna ken a care or fear
Wha hae Him for an ally.

WHEN in the volume of my span of days
I see Time write, towards the end, alas!
My log with storms and troubles never trace
More than a breathing on some polished glass,
I know the wherefore: like some marvellous moth
Gold-chained and swivelled o'er a lady's breast—
Enchanted by her wondrous glory, sloth
Has tranced him captive in his fetters blest,—
So doth my soul within thy beauty bask,
Luxuriating in thy splendrous spell.
No other guerdon ever, ever ask—
To have thee, heaven; to be without thee, hell!
    Fresh'ning its wings against thy lovely eyes,
    The diamond portals of its Paradise.

I MOAN not for the darling buds of May,
Nor Summer's heir, the glorious rose of June,
Nor all the quintessential fruit assay
Of Nature's master-hands, the sun and moon ;
Thou hast the seasons' lovely complement,
Their faint, delicious fragrance merged in thine,
As orient seas are in our sea-shells blent—
Thou hast them all,—and something more divine :
Rare glamours from the far enchanted lands,
Where is no sun nor moon nor light of day,
Nor sound of silver seas on golden sands,
Where lovelinesses herald not decay.
    Earth's beauties, Heaven's joys beyond all price,
    Have consuls in thy wondrous witching eyes.

BELOVED—if no more thy winsome eyes
Should light my pathways o'er this earthly shore,
Nor came again thy sweet, low, soft replies,
Nor witcheries that thrill me to the core,
Nor green apparels of the darling May
Brought thee to share their dear delights with me,
Nor swift enchantments of the Summer's day,
Nor nothing nevermore by land or sea !—
My soul would be as when this world forlorn
Sees not her love, the warm glad sun, arise,
But aches in dreary darkness through the morn,
A grim grey shape along the grim grey skies.
    For thou art to my nature as the sun
    To earth, the longed-for, most adorèd one !

Lo ! as a dumb thing stranded by the waves
Ere they recede to multitudinous shores
Rejoices in his gloomy prison-caves,
When they return greets what he most adores :
So do I count the minutes' ebb and flow
That bear thee slowly, surely back to me ;
And of a surety have I come to know
No freight as precious has Time launched for me !
If there be things that gall the human heart
More than the loss of wealth and what wealth buys,
'Tis from the very dearest one to part—
That one whom you o'er all Creation prize,
    As Earth o'er all created things the Sun.
    Come quickly, then—thou art to me that one.

HENLEY'S INSPIRÈD FAUN

BUT what of those, inspirèd faun,
   Who eat their hearts out in the strain,
Between the darkness and the dawn
   Which in their heart of hearts shall reign?

Who, torn by fierce desire to live
   And love and loaf in sunny bowers,
Bend to the nobler wish to give
   Not riot over virgin flowers?

They, willing Samsons, turn the mills
   That keep the wolf from every door,
Tho' galled by slander's madd'ning drills
   Drown not their heartless world in gore.

But banner high the grand command,
   Their passions barred in iron ward—
'Thou art thy brother's keeper, and
   Against herself thy sister's guard.'

It is not these who sin the most
   Go tear a-muck and ruin all—
The muddy barge in tempest tost
   Still shortens sail at every squall,

To sneak along in devious form,
   And hugs for choice the slimy shore ;
White-breasted frigates dare the storm
   Clean limbed though they return no more.

And yet the world will never see
   An inch beyond its callous nose,
But points and laughs in fatuous glee :
   These Dutch-built lived—but what of those ?

We *do* forgive, inspirèd faun,
   The flaws that made thy life a wreck,
But honoured be the manly clan
   Who seldom bend to passion's beck !

With passionate hearts as strong as thine,
   And brains, if weaker, finer far,
Who have not wallowed with the swine
   But steered their course by duty's star.

Who will not cage his linnet loves
But sets his heart's door wide ajar,
That each may charm the world's groves
And be some good man's guiding star.

Who can give up his dearest ones
And crown his soul in thorns of pain,
Tho' henceforth all beneath the sun's
A murky, weary waste of rain.

Then is the anguish of the heart,
Then is the withering of the soul,
Till loosened be the silver cord
And broken is the golden bowl!

The names are ringing round the spheres
Of such kind, perfect human souls;
For them the angels shed no tears,
They have not missed their manhood's goals!

But where art thou, inspirèd faun?
'Where is thy place of blissful rest?'
Didst *thou* fulfil thy Maker's plan?—
Methinks that silence still is best!

TO MERRIS

It was upon the gloaming hour
    When day from darkness tarries,
I fand mysel' within the bower
    Of my dear lovely Merris.
There were no stars except her eyes,
    Like some fair dove she panted,
I took my heaven by surprise
    And had the bliss I wanted!

I kissed her till the morning light,
    I strained her to my bosom;
Had ever olden king or knight
    A maid or dame sae lo'esome?
And ages lang may come and gang
    Wi' love and laughter laden,
They'll never hae amang the thrang
    Sae rare a night of Eden!

When angels' wings shall hap me round
    And soothe me with their beating,
As comes the grand resurring sound
    Of Paradise's greeting;

B

Tho' glorious be their golden joys,
    Yet I shall aye remember
Wi' fond desire, the sweet, low voice
    Of Merris in her chamber !

CHORUS.

Summer sun or winter snaw
    From Ind to Highland corries,
The fairest, dearest in them a'
    Is my ain darling Merris !

MERRIS'S REPLY

AND by the sacred heavens above,
    I am thine ain for ever ;
Thou never shalt regret thy love
    For me, nay never, never !
As long as life and light extend,
    While earth the ocean carries,
Until the very heavens end
    I am thine only—Merris.

ANSWER TO BLANCO WHITE'S

HOMING to glory, doth our yearning gaze
Not pierce beyond this world to brighter zones,
That rondure with all rainbowed brilliant blaze
Of beauty unsurpassable—the thrones
That mark the grandeur of the King of Kings,—
Shall we abandon dreams of radiant bliss?
Death find us wanly beating phantom wings
Far down some horrent, cold, starlit abyss
For ever?—Leave us yet a thousand times
The faith that, when we die, our caddised souls
Emerge among the golden, rosy climes,
Where the sweet choiring angel chorus rolls
   Unthralled—unjailed—in everlasting day,
   From ghastly, ghostly night and death alway!

COMFORT

Take heart of grace, whoe'er thou art—
Thou still mayst act a noble part,
Tho' thy white soul have many a stain
From hardening lust or cruel gain.
The richest wine has thickest lees,
New life waits on the Easter breeze.
Was traitor ne'er so false and fell
But *one* good woman loved him well?
The shepherd's tale is never told
Till all his sheep are in his fold.
God's fierce electric light could show
Vile blots on all thought pure as snow.
One single hair too much of weight
Can hurl the world from high estate;
One single song, however small,
Can drag whole nations out of thrall.
God's image on the purest gold
Without alloy would never hold;
Howe'er the coin is—battered, thin—
At God's own mint they'll take it in.
Earth's millioned lands of myriad eyes
May hope, like us, for brighter skies,
When blue sky petals fade away
That hide God's everlasting day.

Whenas unlaired the roaring Norther flails
The forest Kaiser, clutching round his heart,
While snows and rains, and sleets and bitter hails
Break many a doubtful root and branch apart;
If he outlast the stormful stress and long
On rushings of the mate-desiring springs
His thinned reviving crests uprear more strong,
Because therein the sun-fraught south wind sings,
So, when misfortune ambushed overtakes
With fiendish claws our cherished pomp and state,
And false friends lour, like Northers charged with
        flakes,
And on our flaws her vials empties Fate,
    We climb, when freed from this proud cumbrous
        load,
    Like sweet new violets peering forth, to God.

HYMN

CREATOR, Lord of Heaven and Earth,
   We render Thee our gladdest praise,
For Thou hast loved us from our birth,
   Hast watched and blessed us all our days.

Secure in Thy protecting grace,
   What are the worst of earthly woes,
The bitter cup, the thorny ways,
   The dire assaults of divers foes?

Thy banner onward still we bear,
   Still be our buckler, leader, friend,
And every danger we shall dare,
   Thy faithful servants to the end.

Father of all, Lord of our love,
   Hear us, poor, humble suppliants :
Thy boundless mercies from above
   Have sated all our earthly wants.

The joys of earth, the world's renown,
   How poor indeed !—When all is o'er
Give us the one supremest crown—
   To be with Thee for evermore !

CHRIST'S CROSS ON HAMMERSMITH CHURCH

THINE awful cross uprears on high,
Athwart the distant Surrey sky,
A magnet, whose increasing power
Through sunny rain or tempest lour
Attracts mine eyes to restful gain
From whirling thoughts in whirling train ;
And once I thought I saw Thee there
When storms were nigh and husht was air,
Dim, as we dimly see the stars
Through daylight's glorious golden bars.
Thy haven cross doth rest the eye
While meaner creeds go whirling by—
Thy haven creed doth rest the soul
While meaner things to Lethe roll.
As murmurings of living streams
Are drowned by passing engine-screams,
Thy truths dim seen, yet unobserved,
Shall keep us right who else had swerved.
When the long train of life is past
Between the platforms clear at last,

When gone are tantalising gleams
And broken glimpses like to dreams ;
When the slow growth of faith is o'er,
Else hollow-hearted at the core,
When Fate, avenger, fills up high
The hemlock of our destiny ;
When Life's grim hurricane is done
And broken both are blade and hone,
When Death has turned the coffin-key
That locks us in eternity,
And Faith, Death's flywheel, 's pulled us o'er
Dead lifts of doubts for evermore,
Us weary wanderers Thou wilt tend
With blissful joys that never end !

As early worms essay the broadened path
In haste to try the tempting wester side,
And find too late the journey perils hath,
And seek in vain their mangled forms to hide—
So country youths forsake their native haunts,
Their humble homes, their hearty, healthy fare,
Their sound, long sleeps, their simply sated wants
Diurnal in the lovely open air.
To some far-off alluring city dream
They crawl, sore bruised and trampled all the way,
Till, mastered by the roaring human stream,
They sink to be some starver, sweater's prey.—
    When will the country learn that cities, wens,
    Are only vast man-eating sweaters' dens?

How the eternal magnets shall sift out
The useless rubbish from the precious grain !
The souls with gold and iron girt about,
Not holiness, shall be withdrawn to pain.
What shall it profit one who owns the world
For some short years of this our human span,
If for all time that comes to be unfurled
He howling lies in Hell beneath God's ban ?
But holy souls, as gluten from the wheat,
The outer husk dissolved, remains behind,
Return, by Death the circuit made complete,
To the eternal living fount of mind.
    Life is but cricket with death's over-ball,
    We players change our places once for all !

THAT beauty can so evanescent prove,
That lovely things should ripen to decay ;
That nothing the cold heart of death shall move
To loose a fair, a sweet, a gracious prey ;
That, ere we reach meridian age, the 'was'
Shall date our dearest friends and foes for ever,
The morning dew still on them, like mown grass
With fragrant flowers between, reblooming never ;
That life be like the perishable web
Of frailest gossamers in pearly Junes,
Or some pure, tender, iridescent bleb
Of tints from far and fairy fleeting moons—
   What strange, kaleidoscopic whirl is this,
   Solvent of early life, and love, and bliss ?

WHERE be the gay green leaves of yester years?
Where be the joyous folk of other days?
All garnered in their long-forgotten biers
We tread a-down the self-same dusty ways.
Ere the sap-vaunting leaves have come of age,
New buds are born that push them off when old ;
Nor gauds nor thrones in this wide world's page
For want of heirs have ever yet grown cold :
This earth in painful parturition brings
The same eternal changeling growths again,
Breast-vaulting from the milky nursing springs
Full-grown—with ages dried up Suns are slain,—
 This world, the sun, the moon, and stars are
  doomed
 To be, like us, in course of time entombed.

If the high, timber-toothed and mighty wheel
That drives a thousand whirling wheels elsewhere
Break but one cog, the others reeling feel
The double impact, till the wheel is bare;
Then rapid artisans, all clanging tooled,
Repair the damage stronger than before,
And where till then the merest whisper ruled
Reverberates the whirring steam's uproar.—
We, reeling from some deadly mental shock,
Can find no artisans to help us rally,
But fiercer yet and faster are we broke
Upon care's wheel, careering down death's valley.
    'Twere wise to put a brake on care and sorrow,
    Shunting them off to never coming morrow.

Thou comest not, nor is it my desire
That my horizon hold thy starry eyes,
To kindle fresh the ashes of love's fire ;
Baffled in reaching what it most doth prize—
As pool-pent salmon longing for the sea,
Lank, lean, and yellow as a wheatsheaf binder,
Remembering well how lusty, silver free,
He waxed as soon as he began to find her ;
Or swallow pining here with broken pinions,
While far away in palm and lotus grove
And gorgeous climates of the Nile's dominions
His mate is mourning sweet her absent love—
   So are my broodings o'er thee, yet for ever
   I will it, that eternity us sever !

For as a marble steeple, reaching far
Among the clouds a slender, lovely form,
When all the elements rise up in war,
Bends like a lombard poplar to the storm,
So cowered I before the blasts of love,
So lost the smiles of heaven from my face.
As undue action ruinates a glove
Did I the holies clustered round my base
For thee, for nothing; thy penumbra lies
Athwart my soul, so frozen chill and chaste
That all the glories of the summer skies
Can hardly fructify the sterile waste.
   Well do I know that with my parting breath,
   Thou, the one-love, wilt come in at the death!

Unbarring dreams of olden, golden times,
Unblurring mirrors of the bygone years,
Restoring youth her lovely summers' primes,
Erasing age his bitter bitter scars,
Bringing the breath of pinelands once again
Across the waves upon the curving shore ;
How doubly dear and fraught with longing pain
Are scenes that we shall see no more, no more !
The darkening, rosy-winged along the skies,
The tendril, churning, creamy lines of spray,
All earth, all heaven in splendid queenly guise
With all the glories of the dying day,—
    And I remember thinking such things are
    Epitomised in thee, my guiding star !

When sixty winters' trains have thundered on
Platforming all our beat, to right and left,
Each quiet, in their cold grave so alone,
Of all but recollection's past bereft ;
While one shred of our body shall remain,
An endless vista fills our mental sky ;
Our lifetime's deeds, through which we Heaven
    attain,
Or Hellward with tormenting devils fly ;
When our last shred of body is consumed
And free to join our soul, our patient spirit
Departs to judgment, cinctured and illumed
By heaven or hell, according to our merit,—
    Oh, it were better we had ne'er been born
    Who only have sown tares instead of corn !

But ere our spirit shall have joined our soul,
The latter, doomed to wander round the world—
Blown in the viewless winds from pole to pole,
By torrid zones or icebergs ever hurled—
Shall see our body's germ of good or evil
Incarnadine with large resultant ill
Or good, vast lands with human wheat or weevil,
For which our soul alone shall face the bill
Of Purgatorial torments, or delight
Far up near Heaven's trancing sights and sounds,
Or in the lowest range in pitchy night,
Or where dim, ghastly twilight most abounds,
    With no companion of our earthly hours—
    Nor bird nor beast, nor trees nor lovely flowers!

Perish the thought!—nay, let me be as trees
Uprooted, branches sunken in the mud,
Flourishing their bleeding roots upon the breeze,
On them straightway emerging leaf and bud ;
So, now my fairest hopes are dead and gone,
Both fruit and blossom buried in the tomb,
Unbalanced, wavering like inverted cone,
By thee ungeared for destiny and doom ;
Yet shall I use the remnant of my days
In helping others up the weary steep,
Diffusing genial, kindly human rays
Of love to dry the tears that others weep.—
    Am I not clay upon the potter's wheel,
    The great Creator's purpose to reveal ?

Judge not the youthful harshly : they are not
To be arraigned with those of riper growth ;
Even such, though heavily with folly fraught,
May finish with some saintly aftermath ;—
For ever yet the goodliest mellow fruits
Have felt the bitter blasting tears of spring ;
Misprisoned April winds that shake the roots
And through the branches icy bullets sling :
The fierce crematings of the July noons,
When breathing only is to be outworn ;
The pensive mildness of autumnal moons
Frosting their likeness on the yellowing corn—
    They who endure, triumphant through it all,
    Are choicer, rarer than some green windfall.

As, to the roaring wester seas, the Clyde
Broad-bosomed floats the barques of commerce on,
And lovely Tweed doth sweetly, softly glide
Unburdened through the eastern leas alone,
Both sprung from the same mighty mountain range :
One, to the fertile east, an ornament ;
The other, westward bearing in exchange
For gold the Cyclops' work wherever sent ;
The singing, sunsmit life was ever thine,
Like Tweed and Clyde we parted once for all,
An atlas-lifting life of shade is mine,
To sad humanity a constant thrall—
    Divided, tortured, drowned in tears, and slain,
    Fate's lobworm bait some wise end to attain.

Lo! as a banknote bears upon its face.
In characters repeated o'er and o'er,
That which doth constitute a solvent grace,
A sponsorship down to the very core—
That otherwise were but a worthless rag
Unfit to light the tiny schoolboys' weeds,
Still less to be a great commercial flag,
Vast emblem of our Nineteenth Century needs,—
So, deep enclosured on the Union Jack,
A thoughtful friend or foe may soon discern
The millioned legions waiting on its beck,
And following all its onward course may learn:
  Fairplay to all has ever been the base
  And bedrock of Great Britain's pride of place.

As iron sharpens iron, so the grand,
Unyielding wrestle of the South and North,
The captives' children from the captor's land
Against their native country issuing forth ;
The mutual respect that foemen feel
For those who front them squarely in the strife,
Inspiring faith, that unioned Commonweal,
To each and all with blessing must be rife ;
Have launched our roster o'er a stagnant world,
Cut the broad arrow on the thrones of kings
Whose tyrant claws have long been sheathed and
    curled
About three-quarters of created things—
    So God's own good from evil ever flows,
    As from dead dung the glorious Dijon rose.

WHEN the vast ironclad's chain anchor breaks,
And like a maddened bull it rams a fleet,
Not through the enemy a course it takes,
But plunges wildly o'er its own *élite*;
Or as the chain that holds the groaning cage
Will snap, and like a flash of lightning sink,
Blotting a thousand miners from life's page,
Through failure of one unsuspected link;
And as one grain of dust will turn the scale
Wherein whole worlds are hung in equipoise,
Expresses find one tiny linch-pin fail,
Smash go the welded steels like brittle toys—
    However small, watch thy least actions well,
    Thy influence may almost crowd up Hell.

For as the frogs in far Van Diemen's Land
Respond to pressures on their brothers here,
And all the years since first the world was planned
Find consummation in the present year;
And all the tremblings of the mighty earth,
In whatsoever distant desert zone,
To some star-golfing Andes giving birth,
Are on the instant well in Comrie known,—
So runs a thrill around the human race
Whene'er Sir Philip Sidney deeds are done,
Or, like Pompeian sentinel, his place
Grand Gordon keeps, to setting of his sun.—
    Oh, then no more poor perishable beasts
    Are men, but guests en route to God's own feasts!

But there is danger, England, far ahead ;
Take lesson from the unconfinèd sea
Within her vast illimitable bed,
And consequently ever salt and free,
Save where the cemetery of lost ships
Stagnates within its narrow dregs and grounds—
Better to hold the world in thy clips,
With generous rival nations in thy bounds.
Scotch, Irish, Welsh, with emulation strung,
Australians, Canucks, Indians, thy best friends,
Had ne'er in brotherhood unto thee clung
Had Edward First attained his selfish ends.
    Rome, proud, imperial, stormed each nation's
        home,
    But smashed in rebaptizing them as Rome !

If God should null the various metals now
And all the precious stones on earth delete,
Tyrants would stamp the image of the cow
Upon the very leaves, ere they were beat!
For poverty breeds ever parasites,
And we shall ever have upon us sorning,
Dark midnight thieves of ignorant people's rights,
That work not square above-board in the morning,
Till, like an unclean salmon in the sea,
The people, pooled in suffering's direst college,
Know what it is to shake bloodsuckers free,
And cleanse them in a perfect sea of knowledge,
    'Neath their slum-floating stone of Burma draw
    New ropes of strictest procreative law.

Trespass not on the helpless, nor on those
Who have against thy strength but weak
    defence :
As peristaltic motions of the floes
Bring up long ages' frozen denizens,
Such deeds will front thee in an icy freeze
Of irresistible, recurrent grief,
When comes the nearing rattle of death's keys
To give thee tenure of thy home in fief;
While, in the long, long watches of the grave
One single integer of thee remains,
Thy soul to hellward fears may be a slave,
Which it, now puffed with foolish pride, disdains ;
    For this is sure, nothing can be undone,
    Howe'er we, wailing, wish it ne'er begun.

MANKIND whene'er their smallest fingers ache
Begin to rail against Almighty God,
And almost by their perturbations wake
The dead, long planted underneath the sod.
Tho' it unto the quantum of their sin
Be as triangle point to sides and base,
God ever is expected to step in
And stop fruition of their wicked ways.
The most ungrateful monster ever known
Is man : tho' Heaven hold him by the hand,
The harvest of his crimes must needs be thrown
Up in God's face, as if 'twere by Him planned !—
    Man ever has been Heaven's thorn and fret,
    And preferentially the devil's pet !

As unsphered swallow in the frozen north
Glides from the darkness through some lighted
 hall,
And wheeling there a while, reissues forth
Into the icy night's funereal pall,
And cannot find the light and warmth again,
And tho' he reach delights of tropic shores,
That one intense contrast of joy and pain
Predominates their sweets and sharp dolours—
So is first-love. Where are the emerald leas,
The lovely colours of the early spring?
The glamours of the multitudinous seas,
Arcadia, where we heard the sweet birds sing?
 Our corresponding heart of youth is dead;
 Love's glories, too, with age's snows are fled.

As the oak-ousting birch, within our years,
Hath climbed through Southern Asia to the poles,
Because no barren stony tract it fears,
Nor shade nor shine can hurt its silver boles,
So will the Asiatic slowly wake
And burst the confines of his stagnant sea,
Making the European nations quake
In terror of the terrors yet to be.
New war takes little heed of bulking thews ;
Its weapons of the newest, direst ken
A child may lead them, and a child may use,
To let daylight through continents of men—
    And worse, a hundred Mongols well can thrive
    On what would not keep one of us alive.

AND wherefore not,—must life spell ever battle,
White brother trampling weaker brother down,
The drums and guns reverberating rattle,
War's laurels thought the only worthy crown?
Strong, savage nations working in the mines
Cursing us victors, while they earn the coins
To pay for huts and gardens, tribute fines,
Prisoned like type within the conquering quoins;
Ever the victors riot on the best,
Until there comes a fiercer, abler race
Of nomads, bursting from the east to west,
That oust such feet of clay from pride of place:
    Does earth get nearer joy and love and peace,
    Or does by hordes the tender-foot increase?

God shall assay the various human race ;
Each colour, in its turn, shall sway the world
In course of time, the others giving place
Even as a full-grown leaf to that upcurl'd.
Ere earth has reached meridian of her prime
The Gulf Stream may again have changed her
    course,
Leaving us in a reindeer iceberg clime,
With all our greatness frozen at its source :
Farewell the hopes of Whites for ever then !
America, with thin Red Indian type,
India, too hot by far to breed white men ;
The Australs, Afric, growing them too ripe—
    As other Europe cannot colonise,
    The world would fall to be the Mongol's prize.

Our prophets sum the evil of our days,
And prophesy the certain course to take,
But who can tell the cyclone's devious ways,
Or what the weather will be when we wake ?
Time only shows the grizzels 'mong the bricks
Of every nation's building—after death
Of those who built,—and if vile plaster-tricks
Conceal the rotten lath and frosted graith
From all the nation daily passing by,
When bulging on repentant dying knees,
What use will be the sobbing millions' cry
To save it falling with the faintest breeze?—
    Wiser a nation is than all its wise
    Collectively, tho' clad in humbler guise !

WHAT will the armed battalion years reveal?
We strain all eyes and ears in vain to learn:
Nor Juggernauts, nor shearing clash of steel,
Nor Janus' Gates, for red lights we discern.
And yet, as long as we shall speak and fight
Straight as the crow flies, which is still our boast,
Doing to all what we consider right,
We shall come out on top, whate'er the cost.
I hold, tho' all the world should say me nay
And laugh within its unbelieving sleeve,
God helps the righteous in their evil day,
And makes it hot for vermin who deceive.
    Onward then, civilising Britain, on,
    Till Gabriel's cease-fire at the final dawn!

SPRING

Why linger longer, tantalising Spring?
We mark thy beacons on a thousand hills;
In crocus flames thy brave advancing wing
O'er towns and downs, and dales and dancing rills;
Thy lambkins run the broose a million strong,
With joy intoxicated bees are humming;
Like rockets show'ring brilliant burning song,
Cloud-spurning larks arise to greet thy coming.
Ere death slips age and care upon my track
And those unerring bloodhounds course me down,
Let me see many a hideous winter's black
Eclipses melt at rustlings of thy gown!
    Thy white-armed clasp invigoration hath,
    And winter brings but ghastly night and death.

When on the mart I view the lazy hours
Creeping to night, like schoolboys at their tasks,
And mark below the trade in sick dolours
Because the world in lovely sunshine basks—
Oh ! then I think how cursedly astray
Our vaunted high-tiled progress !—why should we
Be happy only when the drowning day
Emerges like a spaniel from the sea ?
When mortar-mouthed Bellona laughs with shells,
Found'ring the hopes of nations in their gore,
Making their fertile champaigns, shambled hells,
Where smiling Paradises were before,
    Thriving, we revel o'er the eyes in gold,
    Of states war-ousted from our market-fold.

For as the densest black Tartarean oat,
Tho' stunted, weedy, coarse of stem and skin,
By strong, judicious handling can be brought
To bear the finest wheat, both clean and thin ;
And as queen bees are from the common kinds,
But fed and bred, and sealed and reared apart,
Owing selection to their working hinds,
And, but for luck, had been from rank debarred—
So the grand human points, that make for best,
Are kernelled in the most untoward colts ;
Even as one lordly salmon beats the rest
Of kindred unmaturing parr and smolts,
    Sometimes comes one of royal mental stature
    From out the lowest rung of human nature.

Have I not gauged to rights the world's esteem?
There is no merit now except in clothes;
Aristides is dead, a vanished dream,
Christ friendless, fallen among countless foes,
And bluffing is the only paying game,
Marriage the only twenty-five-foot ring;
Honour and virtue, pureness, manhood, fame,
Beside the horned, golden demon thing;
Man, heaven-cherished, like the adder stings;
Belief in Heaven and Hell is gone for aye!
Yet on injustice, all unerring, swings
The vengeful sword of Heaven, in haste to slay.
    Men's disbelief in God makes them no greater,
    Nor lessens aught our just, all-wise Creator.

How like we traders are to working bees!—
Each one of us may be of royal birth,
Brothers, like them, to queens of high degrees,
Whom fate, not worth, has placed to rule the earth.
Alike through broiling sun and blowing rain
We storm the prizes from their prickly forts,
No humble, fertile flow'ret we disdain,
Useless to us the sweetless rose of courts;
Only the progeny of drones and queens,
Like fatting cabbages, can run to seed,
For overwork, and lack of strength and means,
Misshapes the bones, and stunts and kills the breed.
    When our long toil and strength and summer's
        o'er,
    Our gold-laced wasps burst in and thieve our store.

THE dim horizon lands are ever fair,
Fair is all beauty far across the seas,
Our yearning hopes are ever suing there,
Not here, where we should be on bended knees.
So was it ever—shall be till the end :
Man, compass-like, projects his longing soul
O'er heaven, o'er earth, environing, to wend
In quest to quench at some far-sating goal,
Spiderlike, spinning all from his own core
To span God's vast illimitable deeps,
With spider patience, when God's breath once
      more
His foolish cobweb creeds asunder sweeps.
    In truth man is a gull on ocean brooding,
    Above, below, impenetrable hooding !

WHEREFORE all nature's fighting, fierce unrest?
Survival of the fittest everywhere,
Ducks push their crippled ducklings from the nest,
Unwounded beasts their wounded comrades tear;
Plants also only hold their own by force,
All weak resistance on the globe spells death;
Tho' wheresoever be the planted corpse,
Some vampire thing from it new vigour hath.
Yet when the sun, moon, stars, and earth are cold,
Frozen to solid death our bounding sea,
What matters then who lived or loved of old,
Or what strong monarch held the world in fee?—
    If earth is on a fast-expiring lease,
    Why on earth should not all agree for peace?

Musing within this marble-pillared cage
On the foundations of commercial things,
Cursing the same with daily inward rage—
For by that hinge my future welfare swings—
When I would be among the country lanes,
Watching the world reveal a million-fold
Of fruitage, that shall burst the creaking wains
Before October prinks the woods in gold ;
The upas-tree of man's distrust in man
Towers daily higher, overshading earth;
Our deadly weaponed commerce sits thereon
Rejoicing in all other nations' dearth,
    But Death shall with his skeleton master-key
    Some day reveal the wherefore unto me.

How greater, abler, we than God's dumb creatures,
That cannot speak, or laugh, or make machines!
Where elbow actions form the leading features
To even pressure, giving best the means;
Cathedrals we devise from branching trees;
With lines on cuticle of fingers' ends,
Or horns of rams, we ornament the frieze
And plinths, round which stone vegetation wends,
Ever comparing us with lesser things.
At length we grow so vast in our conceit,
We think our earth the pivot whereon swings
God's all, and we alone are God's *élite*;
    Yet all we see, perhaps, is in God's sight
    A point without or breadth or length or height.

Doth God once hearken to our prayers for coin,
Once look with favour on our earthly schemes,
Fraught with—for gold—a myriad souls' undoing,
Gold far beyond our avaricious dreams ?
Did God plan out this fruitful, glad green earth
To squat a monster nation here and there,
Whereof nine-tenths should daily curse their birth,
Slaving for gauds the other tenth shall wear ?—
On the unjust and just God sends His rain,
Holding no mercies back from bad or good,
But man makes hell of every fertile plain
In aggrandising, shedding brothers' blood !
    Can this go on without a hell hereafter ?—
    Conscience   echoes   Hell's   'no'   'mid   awful
        laughter !

Lo ! all the notes within the range of sound
Are blended in the roaring cataract ;
The lilies resurrecting through the ground,
The baby's coo, the hurricane's impact,
And all the colours underneath the sky
Nestle within the rainbow's lovely span,
And, like a million quivering dolphins, die
In tints of glory—wanner, yet more wan,—
So art Thou present here and everywhere,
And nothing is that is not part of Thee.
When our burnt sun, moon, stars, and earth in air
Float like dead cinders on a heaving sea,
    Smaller than sunbeam'd motes are to our skies
    Are those *our* worlds in God's immensities.

THERE be sad thoughts to thrust at ocean's length,
Sorrows too deep to dare to dwell upon,
That vanitise to naught all human strength,
Yet must be wrestled sometime, all alone :
Better we cannot röntgen future days,
Marching blindfolded up life's gory slopes,
Fate's bastions, and death's ambuscaded ways,
Even to the bitter end of all our hopes.
Could we presage the where and how we part
When this loved one, and that, die at our feet,
Wrung with fell anguish would be every heart,
The feller with the ever shortening leet—
    Life's dial-plate, with such a hideous shade,
    Would be a blank, no progress could be made.

How great was broken-shafted Edward's fury,
Summing what sighted, hated Scotland cost :
Nazareth, all the dearest spots in Jewry,
For ever to the filthy Moslem lost ;
France gone, all England beggared, naught to show,
Seven feet by five of Scotland not yet his.
Has time so pitiful a scene of woe,
A King so humbled in the dust as this?
How Wallace and De Montfort must have smiled,
Fair fighters ever, from their paradise,
To see the underhanded trickster foiled,
Dying, derided by his would-be prize !
    Deceit may snigger ere the fight be past,
    But fairplay does the laughing at the last !

Oh ! how it sickens me to read the rot
About those ancient Greek and Roman frauds !—
One of our men could tie ten in a knot,
Out-art their cleverest, choicest sculptured gauds.
Here, if it paid, new Shakespeares would arise—
In his time fortunes were by poets made ;
Now individual merit starving lies,
Nothing goes down but sordid, swindling trade,
Which, like the hangmen in the olden days,
Samples the best from every soul's possessions—
Hawk-like, preferring their sweet wilful ways
That own no judges, nor no droning sessions.
      'Tween Scylla of still larger syndicates
      We are, and Charybdis of vampire rates.

How the old ways are dying fast, or dead !
The pales between the nations breaking down,
All earthly questions coming to a head,
Bursting like some old Talipash full-grown.
Then law, and gold, and creeds shall be unheeded,
For altruistic fairplay shall be King ;
Such earthy things will therefore not be needed,
Nor even, in course of time, the marriage ring.
Earth, drinking in this glorious larger hope,
As jockey shrinks his faulty weight with wine,
Unballasted of crime no more shall grope
In Cloacas, but rise to heights divine,
    Sinless allowed to sight her port at last,
    God's throne, there to be surely grapnelled fast.

Am I my brother's keeper in the race
For sheer existence? Must I touch down slow—
Restrain my big stride to his cripple's pace,
And help him through life's wolves and winter
  snow?
Take only Bible maxims out to fight
The savage, one hand tied behind my back?
Bury my Greek fire, shells, and melanite,
All science, ere advancing on his track?—
Alas! to gain our very bread we must,
Each time we tear with spade or plough the soil,
Destroy some millions of God's creatures, just,
As much as we, through virtue of their toil.
    God's law this is; but one thing can remain,
    To spare ourselves, and others, needless pain.

Am I my brother's keeper? Oh ! the host
That never are but drags upon us strong !
Riding upon us, whatsoe'er the cost,
Like him that rode the sailor Sindbad long ;
As common cattle cram in an ill skin
Enough to feed a regiment of dragoons ;
With foolscap-folio mouths are ever thin,
And pitching lying tales to doleful tunes ;
And those who callous push them far aside,
Counting them underneath the ban of God,
Are not like us who help them, sorely tried,
Are not like us half clad, half fed, half shod,—
    They, rich, avoid us with insulting scorn,
    We, poor, because we helped the poor forlorn !

WHEN all is done that human brains can do
And we live in the skies or under seas,
All earth, bead-like, is tunnelled through and through,
And we can change the seasons as we please,—
Even then, what are we better than the grubs
That cone-like wrestle on their world, some beast?
Slain with the chafes and rubs of whirling hubs,
Both feasters die upon their waning feast.
What boots man's gory wrestle through the ages,
His never-to-be-satisfied desires,
When the sum-total of the world's pages
Shall perish in the world's funereal pyres?
　　For time shall see our earth, sun, moon, and stars
　　Drop like dead cinders out of Heaven's bars.

God's lovely skies are for the rich alone,
The poor can have no claim or hope therein,
Slummed in close factory garrets, where they moan,
Steeped to the lips in want that breedeth sin.
And so the poor uncloyed die gallows hard,
The rich go smiling in their sleep away—
Nothing has on their roseleaf status jarred,
The poor sin on and starve from day to day.
Be it remembered, all the world's wealth
Is something plundered from the common store ;
The orphans, starvelings, raggeds, out of health,
Are not more plenty now than were before :
   Yet all the time the rich put money by,
   Watching Christ's very own through hunger die !

Wherefore, O rising generation, pause
What sign-posts of thy parting ways denote,
More than the prey from anaconda's jaws—
Once in, there is no backing from Fate's throat.
Life's beer, from battered pewter, beats by far
In flavour, strength, and satisfying vim
Deep draughts from lordly glass or golden jar,
With strawberry-jewelled leaves let in the brim ;
And what fair worlds await us after death,
May be or not, advances upon this :
Where God has made our every moment's breath,
When good and wise, not greedy—seas of bliss—
    This world is Heaven, obeying nature's laws ;
    If Hell, 'tis we alone who are the cause !

Spring, well thou slipp'st the pulley bands on life,
Setting creation whirling round amain,
The stored wheat knows thy rousing drum and fife,
And sweats with keen desire to sprout again;
Huge branches, battered from their parent stem,
Dried up and blackened by the winter's rage,
Bud as if all the world looked to them
For banner-bearers of thy green-leafed gage:
And we remember, with what longing sore,
Far back in memory's dim religious aisles,
As little finger sways a rocking tor,
The love that loosed on us Fate's bitt'rest vials,
    Moving our being, as the deep seas roll,
    In sorrowful wailings of a wounded soul.

WHEN of thy generation few are left,
Thou slowly dying of senile decay,
Like a true steel blade, wearing to the heft,
Too good to let the owner cast away—
What shall rise head and shoulders o'er the rest,
Back looking on thy serried ranks of days,
To gladden thee, as answering to the test
That coming death shows us of Heaven's ways?
The days of soundest body, brain, and soul,
Of heartfelt sympathy with all that is,
Desiring nothing else from pole to pole
That interferes with any other's bliss:
    Sick kings for one day's health, tho' swampt in
        treasure,
    Would barter all such artificial pleasure !

Can we, mere animals, beget a soul?
Nay, that life-germ whereof we are possessed,
That lifts us to some grand immortal goal,
As fire climbs upward, is no more than guest
Led by the hand of God from heaven to earth,
Placed in some warm Atlantis long lagoon
(What time the dry land came to have its birth,
And its huge fluctuant power on seas the moon);
In human molluscs, gaining by degrees
A spine, ribs, hands, legs, hair, and frontal bones,
Emerged they often from those shallow seas
To live in ships, or range the mountain cones,
    And, when Atlantis sank beneath the waves,
    Our missing mollusc-links found deep sea graves.

This earth is not the ante-room to Heaven—
It is a Heaven itself, albeit lower,
And whether any other shall be given
To us, no living human is a knower;
And earth has room for but a single creed,
To suit alike the sceptre, pen, and hod :
' Be grateful for thy life, abolish greed,
Leaving thy future fate and Heaven to God.'
Would we intrust the various railway lights
Unto a pointsman badly colour-blind ?
Will God allow in Heaven, and its delights,
Those who in this, His earth, no pleasure find ?
   Saints who at this, God's earth, but sneer with
      cavil,
   At death will sneak to their own grosser level !

Has God not made our breathing pure delight?
Our food, our sleeps, are perfect every way ;
A feast of lovely colours for our sight,
The moon and stars by night, the sun by day ;
The fertilising snows of winter's time,
The storming rains and driving winds of March,
The warm, reposeful, balmy summer's prime,
Autumn, the season's grand triumphal arch—
Naught wanting that can give a wise man joy.
Yet man, ungrateful monster, beats his breast,
And calls God names, as if He were a toy—
Earth spurning, turns a Heaven hunting pest.
    In all God's works on earth there are no flaws,
    Our sufferings are through breaking nature's
    laws.

Tus, death, how strange that on some day of days
O'er us shall surge a various keen of woe,
From friends, who hear the news with sad amaze,
From foes, who loved us in the long ago.
We shall care nothing for the wordy strife,
The tender last caress, the wreaths of flowers,
Nor nothing never more within this life—
The Sphinx shall not have calmer face than ours :
And shortly, those who mourn us have their day,
Dropping into the sea of vanished things,
And shortly everything shall pass away
Like sea-spray shook from darting swallows' wings ;
    But unto then, fat preachers weave their maps
    Of Heavens, based upon some huge perhaps.

Love is not capital to be repaid
From time to time, and then exhaust for ever,
Nor disembowelled mine on the downgrade,
Whose golden vanished lode returneth never,
Nor mountain tarn, nor oozing river quay,
By lusty suns breast-bared unto the core ;
But, like the moaning of insatiate sea
Pulsing her fierce desires upon the shore,
Sobbing her heart out, longing with complainings,
Shricking in stormy wrath against the skies,
Crowning the earth, her spouse, with all her gainings,
As, ever panting, on his breast she lies :
    This is true love ; and how, sea-sprung, can we
    Love otherwise than our great mother sea ?

My heart bleeds when I think of poets' ends !
After a lifetime's racking misery,
How few and unsubstantial were their friends
To smooth their passage to eternity !
Blinded by Heaven's intoxicating force
Of splendours, which no muck-rake mortals know,
Thereafter is their human intercourse
Smit with unrest, as ocean's ebb and flow ;
And ever comes their constant wailing cry,
Like some lone bittern's in the rainful night,
Protesting how the generations die,
Never to read Jehovah's will aright.
    So poets perish, too too much distraught
    With God, in earthly things to have done aught !

See in long files the gladiators of rhyme
Salute the people, passing on to die,
Unrecognised, unfed, before their time.
' This was our fathers' crime,' our days reply ;
Our later days, no whit behind the old,
Turn down the thumb on every budding bard,
Show'ring on some Barabbas all their gold.
Poetic genius is its own reward,
Until the poet's fine-strung brain gives way
And suicide or madness ends the game ;
Then marble statues rise o'er his dead clay,
And every one finds some one else to blame—
    So it goes on—ever some fresher Keats
    Before the earthy butcher public bleats.

To watch wild beasts of hunger, want, and care
Devour thy poets, thou wert ever first
To gloat above the fell arena there,
Where lay the dying poets thou hast nursed
Thou, Scotland, who denied thy poets bread,
Or work or praise, or aught but sheer neglect.
Tho' thine earth groans with statues to them dead,
Stones—stones for bread—what else could they
        expect?
Dunbar, Bruce, Logan, Tannahill, proud throng,
Dying, salute thy downbent thumb by turns;
Fergusson, Gray, and Hogg, gaunt sons of song,
File past thee—and the shame on 't, mighty Burns!
    His condor soul bleeding, yet soaring higher,
    Strangling twin snakes of lust and low desire.

Thou art a base Chelonian after all !—
She-Judas, Lilith, the Delilah kind,
Vilest of all the women since the fall,
Leaving imagination far behind.
Dost think thy perjury cost me a pang ?
The noblest casting honey-combed throughout
Is yet no better than its useless tang—
Both need refiring for another bout ;
And I can whistle gaily to the breeze
That kisses me, then flies to pastures new :
That and the fickler, wild inconstant seas
Are yet some use more than a maid untrue.
    I will not eat my heart out, die in haste
    For thee, lost diamond that wert only paste !

METHOUGHT I heard great Horace call to me,
Across the intervening waste of years :
'Victorian, what is human life with thee ?
Has thy time greater joys and lesser tears ?
Large loomed the life of Christ to be thy guide,
Machines have lessened toil a million ways,
Earth's produce comes to thee on every tide—
Why is it the millennium still delays ?
All that we thought would make this earth divine
Has come to thee, with benefits unknown,
Undreamt by us, whereof we had no sign.
God has not sent thee backward, but still on ;
    Surely, at last, the centuries go by
    With unvexed ears, no tears, nor needy's cry.'

We have used up thy possibilities,
Man knows too well that he is not divine ;
His hopes of after death delightful days
May be, for aught he knows, shared by his swine.
Still rise the sun, the moon, the stars, and set ;
Still on the world's melancholy shore
Thy baffled sea doth ever chafe and fret
With cadenced, long, reverberating roar,
And still man buccaneers like thine of old—
The name is changed, but we have countless slaves ;
The weaker by the strong are bought and sold,
And hunger-slain, than thine find quicker graves.
   Man's heart since thy time has not changed one jot
   More than the lion's tooth, or leopard spot.

ALL creeds have perished, like a vexing dream ;
Two single, simple germs of faith remain,
Cutting their way through mankind like a fleam,
That starts the life-blood ere one feels the pain.
Our Maker's ways and thoughts are hid from all,
And whether Heaven, or Hell, or none, He fills
With us weak creatures, each a bounden thrall.
We shall go only where our Maker wills.
Can Heaven beat the bliss of this our life,
Where nothing is amiss except ourselves,
'Gainst nature quintain tilting, whose grim knife
Ever upon the tilter deathward delves?
   Who shall make God find us another Heaven,
   We that misuse this one already given ?

As our huge world implies a great Creator,
Our life, our death, without a pain designed,
The Maker than the made being ever greater,
Proves Him all-wise, beneficent, and kind ;
Therefore we wise take all this life can give,
Content to leave it in the hands of God,
Whether again in other stars we live
Or whether ended underneath the sod,
And fortify our souls against the wrongs,
The petty slights, and stabs at life and fame,
Dealt ever to the weaker by the strong
Even Horace now, unto this century's shame.
   God being fatherly, all-wise, and good,
   Why fear?—all is within His amplitude.

AGAIN there comes the agonising cry
Of some rare swimmer on life's iron shore :
' Kind God, is death and calm oblivion nigh
For me, sore bruised, disheartened to the core ?
What homes the swallow far across the foam,
A thousand miles to find a warmer haven ?
What crowns the greatest man as with a dome
Of glory ?—She that Thou to each hast given :
Compared to her naught Paradise's bliss.
Another hath her, nothing fares me well,
My crown of thorns to see her daily his.—
Compared to that, what are the pains of hell ?
       If after death she must be his also,
       Blot me quite out, kind God, 'twere better so !

Why didst Thou furnish me with keen desires,
Immortal longings, never to be quenched?
Trying to save, the surgeons use the pliers,
Soon, soon, the ailing limb is lopped, retrenched,—
Is the man saved from death? Nay! that dead limb
Kills him, by aching, more than all combined.
She hath lopped off my soul to give to him;
Naught earth nor heaven hath is to my mind;
The splendid manhood which was mine by birth
Has served in Thy cause, to the world at large.
But she has wearied me of heaven and earth,
And the long wait that lies between their marge;
    Wherefore, kind God, delete me from all things,
    There is no more whereunto my soul clings.

Dante, shake hands across the grave of years
With me, an exile weary as thyself,
Climbing for bitter bread the narrow stairs
Of those whom fate, not merit, dowered with pelf.
Thy hapless love for Beatrice was not
More fierce, more all-devouring in its rage,
Than that wherewith my whole life has been fraught,
With which determined battle still I wage.
Tho' thou wert spared an insult worse than death,
Thy Beatrice did not mincing pass thee by,
Noting thy quivering lips and tortured breath,
With bitten lip and proud, averted eye.—
    Nay, thine was noble, to thee ever kind,
    Mine had a mounting, Lady Macbeth mind!

AND so my energies are minimised
In stamping out what God Himself put there,
What one had thought a woman would have prized—
A love that owned her fairest of the fair.
Is not the world one reeking shambles now,
To sorrow destined every baby born,
To place upon some baby suckling brow
Ambitious spoils from some poor creature torn?
I have descended from a stubborn race ;
Never shall I betray by word or deed,
Except the hot shame flushing o'er my face,
The slight that me for ever from her freed,
    The stab that pinned one loving soul to hell,
    The slight that pinned the slighter there as well !

When golden slumbers end the weary day,
In dreams again I pace the northern shores,
Whereon the wild, inconstant feminine spray
Kisses the land, or his broad bosom gores ;
Then find I comfort in her lovely arms,
She hath for me no proud averted eyes,
She dowers me then with all her glorious charms,
Sweet amorous kisses, soft delicious sighs,
And there is nothing else to be desired.
No heavens possess a more delightful joy
Than two fond hearts by mutual love inspired,
Pure as the finest gold without alloy.
    Break, break my heart before the dreamer wake,
    Since only she the thirst for her can slake !

Hast thou a woman staunchly, truly kind,
Yielding in thine and her untoward moods? –
She is the noblest thing God ere designed,
Better than great estates, or wealth or goods.
Make much of her, for in thine older days
The glamour shall have faded from thine eyes,
And thou wilt see, with truly Rontgen rays,
How false and coarse the love that money buys.
If, therefore, money buys so little love,
'Tis clear that love is monarch over all
The wealth of which youth cannot think enough,
Chained unto it long weary years in thrall.
   The greatest prize upon this earth is woman—
   I love them all, for I am truly human !

Patience! despised, afflicted, beaten heart,
And rest—thine own shall come in time to thee
Keen as the Crucifixion was thy smart,
For that was short, and thine of long degree.
God's bliss is greater far than all earth's pain,
As God is greater far than His creations;
The martyrs shall a loftier height attain
Than those who brought about their degradations.
She, too, in God's own grand mysterious way,
Shall be refined with sharp and sore distress
In this and other worlds, until the day
She fawns on thee in virgin loveliness.
    Wait thou God's time, by her thy waiting years
    Shall be thick sown with expiating tears.

Has failure met thy cherished long desire,
Slain it upon the setting of thy sun,
Leaving thy heart a broken, tuneless lyre,
For what in life can be but once begun?
Thou mayst have answered all the calls of Heaven;
The fairest colours of the lovely rose
Are not the petals by the day-god riven,
But those that she deep in her heart doth close;
The finest, most aspiring thistle-down
Is blown upon the roadways, rocks, and seas,
The wingless, heavy, common sort are sown
And thrive in millions, in their native leas.
   'Tis not thy merit, but the will of God,
   That plans thy beat till underneath the sod.

O SWALLOWS, lingering o'er the telegraph-wires
In serried thousands for the final flight,
God sates with full fruition your desires!—
Ye have no freezing, dark December nights;
Your pathways o'er the seas are as of old,
Before the waves the leas asunder tore;
At dawning here, at dusk your wings ye fold
By some warm Nubian lotus-laden shore.
Could I escape, like you, to rosy climes,
Far from the coming autumn of my soul!
Nor you, nor I, repeat the glorious times
All have before they sight their final goal!
    Columbine springs shall dance thro' life's trap-door
    Long after we return no more, no more!

A, man-like, blindly falls in love with *B*,
A love that deeper grows with lapse of time :
B, woman-like, reciprocates, but she
Thinks she may well have other birds to lime ;
Wherefore by turns she weds the alphabet,
Except poor *A*, who takes to making money.
When she has urned them—not to their regret—
Herself then old and thin and scant of honey,
She thinks that after all *A* was the best ;
The love whereof he has been long demurraged,
Her burnt-out fires with feeble, eager zest
She gives—the millionaire must be encouraged—
    Herself—toom eggshell—with a regal air,
    And thinks—how just !—that she has made things
    square.

G

As when a gallant horse goes down for good
And breaks his trappings, kicking unto death,
Till some bystander of a kindly mood
Sits by his head, and calms his lab'ring breath,
And frees his harness, helping him to stand,
Adjusts his collar gently on again,
Patting him meanwhile with a soothing hand,
That robs this life of half its galling pain—
So is it when a business man goes down
Through a gross combination of mishaps:
If he be helped before he gets too blown,
Brilliantly will he finish off life's laps.
    Fate's rod is growing now for each and all,
    Wherefore be kind to others in their fall.

SHE glances in the crowded train for room,
Then Heaven enters in with her for me,
Transfigurating all my lifetime's gloom.
As night the moon, into a silver sea,
Parted so long, to part again so soon,
This time, alas, alas, for evermore!
My life has but this solitary June—
Her mouth its roses—on this earthly shore,
And I within the dungeon-bars of fate
May look and long, but never trespass there ;
As the sun glories down the wester gate
She goes, she leaves me darkened with despair,
    Like one long dead, seeing through all his past
    Two amber eyes that light alone its vast.

Nay ! flaunt her on her low Chelonian range,
Without the finer feelings bought with tears—
At such a price I would not have her change ;
Prometheus-like, give me a million years
Of further anguish.   What is pain to me
Beside the agony that would be mine,
The ever-fleeting, reconstructing sea
Of grief to know that grief touched her, my shrine ?
Nay ! as the nines breed ever fresher nines,
However complicated be the sum,
So love is ever based in Thy designs.
Great God, and somehow Thou wilt make it come.
    Death, cleanse her from all tainted stud desires,
    My soul teach hers love's purest, loftiest fires.

FORGET her! as a picture's lovely key—
Some rare Madonna face in early times,
Ere art had moulted wings, unfettered, free,
When Raphael, Angelo, were in their primes—
Is blighted, and our days cannot repair,
More than put keenest edge on copper blade,
The damage envious time has painted there,
And the sweet vision is allowed to fade,—
So my life wants its holy centre-point ;
The cows, the sheep, the trees are all around,
But she who did the whole with Heaven anoint
Is but a phantom on a phantom ground—
    Gone she that me for loss of all sufficed,
    And going surely with her is the Christ !

As when the plough untombs an ancient coin,
And gathering round the busy, wond'ring swains
Find it too thin, too worn for their knowing,
Whether or no 'twill add unto their gains,
Till one shall heat it fiery red, and then,
Clear to the dullest vision, can be seen
By whom, what for, the value, where and when,
Also the image of some lovely queen—
So I forget thee not as I wane old,
And near the confines of my furthest shore
The rosy flush of love upon the gold
Of me reveals thee driven to my core.
        Time, garner all within thy bending sweep,
        But let the one love to my bosom creep.

THE voice of him that loved her best on earth,
Within her silent chamber all alone,
Or flaunting 'mid the high-born halls of mirth,
Or where the seas make melancholy moan—
Will it not come with haunting emphasis,
A guest unbidden, yet at all her feasts,
Rising between her and her husband's kiss
With mournful eyes, like those of tortured beasts,
Pleading for mercy, yet too proud to speak?
What could true manhood do but turn away
When slighted?—only curs would vengeance wreak!
The voice of him whose soul she tried to slay,
    Like Christ's with Pilate, shall with her abide
    For ever, missing neither time nor tide.

'THERE is a tide which, taken at the turning.'—
What of the battered wrecks upon life's shore,
That some unprecedented spring-tide, spurning
The skies, had hurled inland for evermore?
The marshal's baton in the soldier's kit
Will not prevent the bullet through his heart ;
Life's seas have not been navigated yet
Save on the lines of Providence's chart.
Seeing the cross afar off from the side,
You scout the feeble ones who bear it ill,
But God thought they were worthy to be tried.
And you so lofty He may reckon nil :
　　Wherefore, treat not the poorest with disdain,
　　For they, not you, eternal life may gain.

WHENE'ER I hear this author makes his pile,
That poet blows his trumpet far and loud,
I smile unto myself a quiet smile,
And lose myself unnoticed in the crowd.
For them, poor parasites, it is enough
To owe their bread unto the public favour,
Whining like lapdogs at the least rebuff!
The bread I eat, my body's labours pay for;
My laboured brains within the mart's arena
Helping the sacred cause of commerce on—
Let the *haute* world take careful *nota bena*,
That is this nation's very frontal bone.
    I rank far up the vast poetic clan—
    Better, I take high rank as able man.

Have I not been through life a hunted bear,
Naught to depend on save myself alone—
Whom every should-be friend has tried to tear,
Whose nearest blood relations bid begone?
With thy fell dart, dear love, driven to my heart,
Sapping my weary vitals more and more,
Have I not rent life's jungle far apart,
Tho' every step made wider yet my sore?
Despite of thee and all the hounds of chance,
And fate, that coward-like rips me behind,
I have not stinted aught my fierce advance,
I am no feeble-to-be-daunted hind;
     I joy in proving one of manhood's best,
     Right in the teeth of life's own fiercest test!

Say, England, is it wise, this fiery fight
For sheer existence in this land of thine—
Where traders only get the meanest bite
Working as hard as any former nine,
Where grapes from France, and oranges from Seville,
Fresh fruits and meats from all the world, the best
Make even the poorest little children revel,
And after stand out manhood's fiercest test?
There are no third wheels in thy national cart,
No cog-wheels fitting on a toothless cam,
No imbeciles within thy nation's mart,
No sentiment but the eternal *quam*.
   Yet it is wise ; this battling breeds a race
   Pre-eminently for the topmost place.

She opens not the railway carriage-door;
Westminster comes and goes, but never she—
Perchance she will return no more, no more,
And with her goes my Heaven's only key.
In place of her, my Heaven, sits Hell's fuel,
Cramming the first-class with their purse-proud faces,
As when a glazier's cutter drops its jewel,
And looks, tho' strong, the type of all that base is.
How cursedly fate engineers the race!
Her perfect cylinders make victual-tubs;
Her perfect pistons take the crowbar's place,
And soon go under with the blows and rubs—
    And yet, the world's prize-winning destined nation
    Is that whose sons count self a mere negation!

How the vast panorama of our days
Is marching with us to a looming end,
Thinning by various droppings on the ways
Of many a bitter foe and faithful friend!
And the great host that started stride by stride
With us has dwindled to a painful close,
Like some tall pennon that has long defied
The combined onslaughts of a million foes!
And presently the world and all its cares
Shall rave above our unconcernèd heads ;
No thrones shall interfere in our affairs
Nor make us raise our heavy weighted lids.
    A wastrel, being dead, is greater far
    Than saint or king that has not crossed the bar.

Mark in the panorama of our street
The various passers with their various pace :—
Loafers, their arms recurring like four feet,
As if on fours they would themselves debase ;
The joiner drives a constant unseen saw,
The plasterer holds aloft one brawny hand ;
Policemen keep hauling prisoners to the law
In their mind's eye, as on their beat they stand ;
Well-dressed, the pound-a-weeker clerk is there
With starving, mutinous face and spider legs ;
And wealthier far, and freer yet from care,
The tramp, who has a pitch and sweeps and begs,—
    Ambling through all, the parasitic they
    Well off who never toiled a single day !

WHEN I observe the scarlet-runner plant
Pinched of its pods ere they have fully riped,
Begins new banners everywhere to flaunt,
Like us when our battalions are outwiped;
Then do I see the type of all that is
Most admirable in this world of ours,—
The constant war to better what's amiss,
The hapless fight against the stronger powers.
How the same plant sends out, when left alone,
A pod or two, luxuriating, content
Thereafter till its summer life be gone,
In useless leaves and tendrils o'er the bent.
    So man, pinched, bruised, and baffled every way,
    Works like a giant, not a child at play.

YET, after all, it is the man himself:
No externalities can alter much
Whether he yield, tho' dowered with fortune's pelf
Or not, to common sense's slightest touch.
Unless the saint and animal in him
Are equal, like divided head of screw,
Fate, driving home with her screw-driver grim,
Will splinter him, because he is not true,
And saint or beast alone is little use
When tottering human bonds must hold together:
So badly balanced men are but refuse,
No good for even their own summer weather.
  A man with warp or bias in his ways
  No headway makes in these our fighting days.

WHAT work does labour, and what work does wealth?
The two can best be sensibly compared—
Presuming both have grown to perfect health,
And both have just begun to wear a beard :
The gentleman lifts weight as the cube root,
At times, to keep himself in good condition ;
The labourer lifts its product, and, to boot,
Goes quickly, surely, to workhouse perdition.
Is there a difference between man and man
That justifies an ending like to this ?
It never was in the Almighty's plan ;
But wicked mankind drives God's plans amiss,
    Looting his brother as if God-empowered,
    Defying all the hells that ever loured.

H

Thou, England, with the calm, victorious brow,
What is there in thee that we Scotsmen stand,
Once foes, now friends, more fierce to guard thee
    now
Than when we fought thee for our native land?
A wrathy race, who wins our long regard,
May safely print it on the rising sun,
That something near to the impossibly hard,
Winning the Scots love, has at last been done,
And thou hast done it.   Let old England fall
Or be in danger, quick round her would sweep
With furious rush a Scottish warrior wall,
Would high to heaven old England's banner keep,
    And this, too, while one kindly Scot had breath,
    Else with his English brother fall in death!

'THERE was an idol that had feet of clay.'
What words can harrow more a loving soul—
For to most lovers comes an awful day
When that shall topple from the pedestal—
As when a weary mariner at sea
Beholds a mirage of some desert waste,
Where every step doth plunge one to the knee
In sand, with ribs of men and camels laced?
So in the soul's gaunt mirages of hell
There ever bends a shrouded, weeping form
Above some broken idols, where they fell,
In grief's own agonising, surging storm—
    As easy change the colour of our eyes,
    As raise our idols from their fallen guise !

Dost thou deride my long years' non-success—
Thou, first, best motive power unto my wheel?
And how much more I could have done, not less,
Thou being kind, the judgment shall reveal.
'Tis easy, being reared within a ring
Of rich relations, forcing one along;
A poor man, wanting these, must be a king
Of men, who storms to front rank, being strong:
But I was neither, only racer build
And blood, that tires the coarser unto death,
Abandoning no purpose unfulfilled
While the tired heart and soul one effort hath;
    Even with this galling ice upon my heart,
    Thou, God-sent mate to me, didst but desert.

WHERE shall this chrysalis of mine be laid
When I am done with it for evermore?
Within some huge cathedral's gloomy shade,
Where all is solemn, stately, chill, and frore;
Or in some far God's acre, where the soil
Is rarely vexed for years, with our young dead,
And our long dead hear not the voiced turmoil
Of some live city, roaring overhead?
Nay! as the lady-birds, that cling beneath
Some damson branch, would be my final lair,
For they emerge in time a lovely wreath
Of sweetest blossom, fruit, and foliage there.
 This were betimes a nobler, lovelier end
 Than worshipped dust, where passionate pil-
  grims wend.

Easy it is, relations all around,
Ever to go the right way, not the wrong;
Religion, morals, conduct, creeds all found,
Like a roped tiger, wend they safe along—
Should one side fail, the tiger rends the other.
Ill fares the youth entirely left alone
Without a father, worse without a mother,
For much in after years each must atone.
The world allows no discount from his debt,
But adds unto it all the father's sins;
One has to pay, with compound interest net,
The lot before his happiness begins.
    Does it begin?   The world is quick and cruel
    To make more martyrs, and to find the fuel.

But are not women strangely like the moon,
Their mother, in her various moods of change?
Not with us in the business blaze of noon
Night shows, from pole to pole, her wondrous range,
There is no warmth in her brilliant light ;
Who stands her smiles offguard, finds madness there,
And shortly knows himself in blackest night,
Cursing himself betimes, in his despair,
Because she seeks some other fools to lure—
Must have them all, not leaving even one.
And when, poor fool, he thinks himself secure,
Again she comes, again he is undone !
    And foolish man may dream, and hope as soon
    To sway one woman as to sway the moon !

To know oneself a gem, unrecognised,
That should be worn upon the breast of beauty,
Whose love more than a million worlds is prized,
For whom to storm to fame becomes a duty ;
To know oneself the bright, particular star
Of all the centuries, in grip and brains,
Paling all others to the milky bar,
That heaven's vault with feeble flicker stains—
To know all this, with equal power to feel,
As Shakespeare felt, with his recondite mind,
That genius is as sportsman's dog to heel
Of coin ;—for him or lesser stars to find
   Some fortune-dowered dolt their charmer hath,
   Is bitterer than the bitterness of death !

A CHILD of Hagar !—when will mortals learn
The curse of God is not on such as these !
But, as a thoughtful eye will soon discern,
'Tis on their foes, in various degrees—
Nay, those who have no earthly father, gain
An awful champion in the God above !
Note how their tyrants everywhere are slain,
How those who scorn the orphans lose His love ;
How presently, tho' men of good estate,
They seem to dwindle into evil ways,
And their descendants recognise, too late,
God sums the father's sins in different ways.
    The Pharisee who flaunts his moral creed,
    Will find Hell snatch him very quick indeed !

Mark how the times are in a frightful coil,
Like when an eel has ravelled up the line
And hung itself : so do the sons of toil
When they against their masters' will combine ;
When Tweed runs clear, and Teviot dark as blood,
Who marks that fairest scenery on earth,
Till under Kelso Bridge the married flood
Rolls—burnished silver—crooning, cadenced mirth.
If the tired piston, labouring up and down,
Refuse to enter more the cylinder,
That moves not—all is lost.   Let them have grown
In unison, each doing its own share,
    Makes yet the only plectrum that can roll
    Immortal music from the British soul !

Oh, 'tis a hateful age !—'twas better far
In the old times, by stalwart clash of arms
To take the lady in the din of war,
And not, as now, gaze helpless on her charms.
What joy to hew the base deceivers down,
Who would have sold her for the highest price ;
To spoil, to sack, to fire their cursèd town,
What angry lover would let less suffice ?
These days are parted, *au revoir* ; our days
See life a sack-race, where the bold go down—
The mean—the sneaks—the wrigglers—win the bays,
And blood is nowhere with the plough-foot clown.
    We are a wobbling, sordid, muck-rake lot,
    For whom no hell can ever be too hot !

THE brood of Pharisees will never die ;
They judge not, like a jury, on the acts,
But some low viper starts a hue and cry
Of lies those base resetters fuse to facts,
Until some noble, spotless souls are slain,
Boycotted, by the would-be godly good—
For nothing can remove the vitriol stain
Of their vile point-the-finger attitude.
Batrachian Pharisees, uplift your eyes,
Resetting scandal at Belshazzar feasts,
More low by far than your own low-browed spies
That carry tales, and thereby prove them beasts :
      See to it !—meddle not with others' falls,
      Hell's finger writes your doom upon your walls.

GREY hairs, of what are you the harbingers,
Ere youth has touched the noontime of the day?
Are you celestial, silent ministers,
To warn us that we are not here to stay?
Or have we given way to base desires
That drove the life-blood to its citadel,
Leaving you outworks ashen from the fires
Of some strong love, not wisely but too well?
And yet, to gain the glorious heavens above,
At death one question shall be asked, not more:
How many, and how deeply, didst thou love?
For God forgives and loves all, o'er and o'er.
    As base love makes our hearts of life be wrung,
    So pure love makes us ever ever young.

.

THE raw material from the stalwart north
Will make the steeliest tempered blades alive ;
Caught young, exiled afar to battle forth,
They cut through all, and make thee, England, thrive :
But left at home—that overheated hell
Of oily priests and canting, whining knaves,
And sawdust creeds—they turn a softened sell,
That nothing on the world's record graves.
Thou, England, with thy disadvantages
Of milder climate, smaller, slighter breed,
Hast yet no monster churches, with their knees
Pressing thy windpipe till thy nostrils bleed—
    Thou hast fought free from sacerdotal bands,
    And art the bravest land of all the lands.

THE human hand can take up molten lead,
If handled at the rightful stage of heat ;
So are there times in earning daily bread,
That puzzle even the best experts to beat.
Unhandled right, our Sphinx-like times devour
The failures, as the dead far out the sea,
And fresher sandbanks in life's business lour
Than our forefathers ever dreamt would be,
And only bought experience can suffice
To bring our business cargoes safe ashore.
A temperate life—a will like iron vice—
Resourceful—honourable to the core—
    Even then some unexpected cyclone rises,
    To bottom sends the best men's best devices.

WHY should the poet be a thing apart,
A watcher of the battle from afar,
Singing from empty mouth, not deep, full heart,
Of all the perils that attend life's war?
Can he not be as modern jumping bean
That carries its own motive power within—
Not as Batrachian, slow, however lean,
Propelled by volts upon the hinder skin?
Can he be guide, philosopher, and friend,
To lead, to soothe, encourage for the best,
Who is a gilt-edged nego, vile fag end
Of courts, unputtable to manhood's test?
   Better, Petovi-like, with dead braves lie,
   Or, Horace-like, to leave one's shield and fly!

The self-same day whereon thou readest this,
Or whatsoe'er thy fancy may dictate,
Will come some year, and get nor no nor yes
From thee, to aught inspired by love or hate ;
For thy time shall have come for other spheres,
Beyond thy power to hasten or delay.
When that time comes, in vain shall be thy tears,
Entreaties, prayers as vain—thou must away ;
Thy beauteous fineries for evermore
Thou shalt lay by for fashion's gilded chains,
And all the vanities in fashion's store
Are vain, where everlasting silence reigns :
    Thy heart-beats are life's going, going, gone !
    Death bidding, bidding steadily, alone.

A DREARY, dreary look the ocean hath
Tasselled with seagulls, far away through mist:
The long shores thick with heaps of stranded death,
All living things unto the sea are grist;
And looming ghastly, ghostly in the rains,
The while the fog-horns roar like maddened bulls,
Seen dimly, as through darkened window-panes,
Are the huge warships' towering, louring hulls—
And this is all: there are no crowded throngs,
Swaying and pushing, on the silent pier,
Braying with brazen throat their asinine songs,
The gay world throngs not to the funeral bier.
    Of all the months, December, lord thou art,
    Thine icy fingers close upon their heart.

AND I have touched the keystone of the bridge
Of life, and feel that I am growing old,
And rising gaunt before me, ridge on ridge,
The peaks are ice—not warm with summer's gold ;
And all the chattering daws that prate of age,
Lie like the crafty fox that lost his tail—
And lies will not one single pang assuage
When we are ageing, therefore growing frail.
What comfort is it when one walks the plank
Of life, to know we go not there alone?
And wherefore should we give a single thank
To know this world in death's waves shall go down?
    Our only comfort is, our Maker knows
    What's best for those He loves—and we are those.

What earthly yearner gains the full desire,
The ripe fruition long so panted after?—
The poet tries to sweep his own heart's lyre,
And finds the pathos woven in with laughter;
Quicksilver thoughts that tell the passing hour
He seizes, but to find them flit away
Around him in a broken, baffling shower,
Beyond his most importunate assay;
And the deep soul of beauty none can reach—
Only her garment's hems are kissed by few,
And these can seldom render into speech
A fragment of the ecstasy they knew
    When first, like visions of the Holy Grail,
    She burst on them in shining, lovely mail.

Oʜ for an extra muse to help me o'er
The steep inclines of modern thoughtful ways,
For in the dark December days, how sore
To make some verse that time shall not erase !
Vain is the wish !—No Chapman ever can
Continue Marlowe's verse with Marlowe's grace ;
And every poet, so he be a man,
Need borrow no thumbs from his fellow race ;
The more his features rise in bold relief,
The deeper shall their shadows surely gloom :
Wherefore, waste not thy breath in idle grief
O'er poet faults when he is in the tomb,
    But laud his music—march—and stately ring,
    Thanking the Lord you have so grand a thing.

How did he make the keen Ferrara blades,
That beard, till now, the storm and stress of war,
And beat, when matched in Oriental raids,
Their best for tempered excellence by far,
Tho' many a hundred years have gone since he,
Their maker, filled an exiled Scottish grave,
Carried from snows where he toiled to the knee
In dim recesses of some Highland cave ?
And so the man who hopes to pierce the heart
Of Time, and grave a lasting message there,
In poverty need school his soul, and part
From all this empty world considers fair,
    And in his lifetime none shall thank him aught,
    But hold in high derision all he taught.

How much the self-tormenting spirit aches,
Ever inventing lions in the path !
No ill has happened others, but he quakes
For fear the same thing for him fortune hath.
The longer he escapes, the more he sees
With certainty the coming avalanche
Of miseries that shall bring him to his knees
And smash him up, both root and stem and branch.
Yet, as a weakly man lives longer far
Than those who have some stamina in hand,
Who set their nerves and fibres all ajar,
Plunging for every pleasure in the land,
    So caution seldom gives itself away,
    While reckless rushers always fang their hay.

But thou, named after the Madonna, wert
The sole possessor of my heart and soul ;
Tho' others may reclaim my surging heart,
And with breakwaters levy scattered toll,
Yet, as the sea rebels, and skyward sets
Protest on bounds with every shuddering wave,
So all the ocean of my being frets
Rebelliously toward thy lonely grave.
Is there no 'lembic on this earthly shore
To join fond lovers to their wonted weal ?
Quicksilver draws to it its dusty ore,
Each plastic, joined, they hold more true than steel.
    Tombed by great Cheviot thine enchantments lie,
    That mateless hold my soul until I die.

Our lives are full of endless sacrifice,
And much is done that never meets reward.
All men, however shrewd, however wise,
Will often find their best endeavours marred
By something coming at the eleventh hour
That never happened since the world began,—
For we are subjects to an unseen power,
That passes or rejects our able plan
For some wise end, as time shall yet reveal ;
We are but cruising to death's unknown seas
Under sealed orders : death shall break the seal,
To port us where the great Commander please,
   And all we hope, or think, or do, or say,
   Will steer us not the least from God's own way.

Economy!—oh hateful, hideous word,
Sole cause of sufferings to the human race!
They who have rusted have much further erred
Than they who wisely well have gone the pace.
The peasants cheat themselves of generous food
And die untimely; the mechanics, too,
Leaving behind a pinched and meagre brood
Of sickly dwarfs, who find no work to do,
And these breed others, weaklings, till the swarm
Of ill-skinned mongrels threat to fill the earth :
'Tis not their fault, but they are only harm
To any country, being nothing worth.
    For God's sake let us have some newer light,
    And tomb that dead, ripe-rotten word from sight !

WHAT is the poet?—nothing but a freak
Of Nature, with twin souls instead of one—
A lion man and tender woman, meek,
Joined in one body, as a man alone.
Each one predominates, will rule the verse,
From grave to gay, from dancing to severe,
Diffuse, expansive—witty, crisp, or terse,
Will rouse the wrath of man or woman's tear.
Should both be balanced, wide will be his range.
Chameleon-like his rapid change of mood ;
His looks, his conduct too, will be as strange,
And of prize-oxen boors ill understood,—
    To measure such by common folk is vain.
    For dull, thick-headed goodness is his bane.

'Tis better far to wear out, than to rust
In lazy, gouty, ignominious ease
Before the wine of life has gone to must,
A mass of undistinguishable lees,
A bitterness to self and all around,
That can give pleasure to no living creature—
That even the sun would wish were underground,
As destitute of all redeeming feature.
Better the bright brave blade that breaks in war,
And saves a country by his bold example,
Than gourmet keeping peaceful doors ajar
With feeds for him, that were for ten men ample.
    Through gluttony imperial Rome went down,
    And the reverse gives Germany a crown.

And is it doomed to be a last farewell?
Shall nothing reinstate love's ruined gap,
Through which our seas of tears pour, making hell
Of our two young lives to the farthest lap?
Though each encounter in the after days
Sweet other loves that may be twice as fair,
How tame with us the raptures they can raise,
And each of us will want the other there!
The turbine of our love is drowned in tears,
Only we two combined can set it right:
Oh, then let us unite for brighter years,
Not sever unto love's eternal night—
    For, as leviathan loves but the sea,
    So is my deepest love alone for thee!

When the end comes, and all is o'er for ever,
When life's delightfulnesses are no more ;
When I shall have to ford the deep, dark river
Of death, in hopes to reach the heavenly shore,
What shall be my reception ?   Will the tones
Of grand, immortal music fill my soul ?
Will there be countless glittering, splendid thrones,
Whereon for ever to recline and loll,
Finding but one supreme delightfulness
In letting pleasure drift in to the core —
One of a mighty, mazy wilderness
Of angels, who do nothing but adore
    The Highest, veiled in glorious misty screens,
    To mercifully tone His awful sheens ?

THINKING on this, I fell asleep, and dreamed
An angel set me high upon a peak
Above the plains wherethrough death's river
    streamed,
To note how Azrael doth vengeance wreak.
The river was deep, dark, and turbulent,
With angels good and bad upon its shore—
Being one's earthly good or bad deeds, sent,
Not lost, but waiting for one on before.
Self-abnegation counted here for much,
Wealth, rank, and title did for nothing tell;
I saw the kindly buoyed up into touch
Of Heaven—the selfish swept away to Hell;
    One's least kind action proved an angel strong,
    A fearful demon one's slight wilful wrong.

And lower down before the cataract
Of Hell were creeks and level swamps, where lay
Those who missed Heaven, thence with anguish
    racked
Would have in sound of Heaven and Hell to stay.
Women were there, who loved an early love,
And by them were beloved in return ;
But rank and gold and jewels did them move,
And so their God-sent lovers did they spurn.
They hear their lovers calling them from Heaven,
They hear their children cursing them from Hell—
Their darlings, whom to tortures they have driven,
Keen agonisings horrible to tell ;—
    Yet for them unallowed to expiate,
    More terrible than damning is their fate.

How is it that between the man and beast
Exists a strong resemblance ?   Can it be
That in God's chain the latter is but least,
And nearly human in a less degree—
That when the darkness which o'erspread the earth
Uplifted in one spot, all tried erection
On two feet, as we humans do from birth ?
Not needing to go head-first for protection,
So all these creatures gradually grew human ;
Elsewhere a million years the darkness reigned,
So no more creatures grew to man and woman,
But stereotyped to all-fours they remained.
    This guess may not our missing link supply,
    And how we came I care not, no, not I !

BETWEEN unequals, sweet is equal love :
That may be so, but it will never hold,
For, be their status more than one remove,
And nothing can prevent them growing cold.
True : frosted iron burns like that red-hot,
But 'gainst the cold gives out no gentle fires ;
So two unequals may love well, yet not
Be actuated by the same desires.
Congenial moods to one may quench the other ;
Summer kills ice, and winter summer's heat,
Far as the poles they are from one another.
Only in point of burning do they meet ;
   But those whom truest love hath ampersanded,
   Will never find the marriage countermanded.

That there is good and evil in the world,
Is quite as patent as the world itself.
If evil comes through being over-churled,
Or good from being overstocked with pelf,
Or whether mankind, like a seidlitz, would
Be bad when only one of two compounds,
Or need to be monotonously good
Or bad, we have not quite sufficient grounds;
But, as a tree puts forth a stronger root
For anchorage upon the windy side,
So active evil raises an *émeute*
Of goodness, to crush down the evil tide.
    The moon of goodness holds in check the whole
    Of evil's rising tides, from pole to pole.

'Tis vile that we should ever have to age
And leave behind the dear delights of youth,
To near in our life's book the final page,
And face the glaring but unwelcome truth :
To leave behind the merry, merry laughter
Of when we were too young to have a care,
And the grey-bearded roar that lifts the rafter!
Maids laugh like wine gurgling from beakers rare,
Saddest to us we stalwarts dwindling small
Through age, as when a moving railway train
Shrinks up till it is hardly seen at all,
Or looks a crawling speck upon the plain.
    Sad tho' it be, we must in time give way,
    And our heirs too will age and have their day.

Thou wilt not mourn for me when I am dead,
Thou wilt not waste one silent, single tear
Upon the narrow, all-sufficing bed
That shall be mine for many a lonesome year.
Oh, wherefore should my soul be sorely versed
To chronicle the fact of thy disdain,
But that a burn, straightway in heat immersed,
Writes off instanter something from the pain !
Thou shalt in time be spancelled too by death,
And none or few shall dream of mourning thee—
We mourn the loss of her alone who hath
Been kind to all, without reward or fee.
  As lungs of miners petrify to stone,
  Hard hearts go hardening slowly into bone.

England, no deep-toned octaves nor no shrills
Are thine, as with us too perfervid Celts,
No storm peaks, nor no sylvan rippling rills ;
Calm is thy life as are thy rolling veldts ;
Thy sons have not our frenzied, furious dash
That storms to battle, like our Highland gales,
But on with steady bayonet's deadly clash,
Nor count the foes, nor heed the bullets' hails.
Not much thou troublest over future states,
Content to show a manly break in this ;
Nor whinest on deathbeds for huge rebates,
But hop'st that God will not forget in bliss
    Thine who have faced their punishment in strife,
    And never sneaked behind with coward knife.

Doth not the earthquake and the lightning kill
Alike the good, the bad, and those too young
To be presented with life's evil bill,
For which their spirits should be surely hung?
And is not this a chance to rail at God
For something that mankind can not prevent,
Not making the catastrophe be slowed,
Not picking only out the malcontent?
That flash, that earthquake, would have smashed
    the earth
At any other time and place ;—the few
Who perished then in Heaven will have no dearth
Of extra bliss, and have no hell to do.
    God, who can balance all the worlds in air,
    Can be depended on to play us fair.

O THAT it were eternal summer here !
What use our constant rain, and frost, and snow ?
They say it sweeps the fields and pastures clear
Of larvæ—breaks the clods, and makes food grow.
But in the Channel Islands, where the frost
Doth rarely touch the tender, dainty flowers,
Of ten times more luxuriance can they boast,
Grand fruitage, flowers, and foliage than ours.
And if our freezes whet the appetite
Of some, with cupboards high in good things piled,
Think of the poor with pantry unsupplied,
Thin, ragged, shivering, even in winters mild !
   Winter of after death the mirage is,
   Summer is that of never-ending bliss.

There is a love that ends in sacrifice,
However fiercely felt the self-surrender,
Tho' shame and agony may be the price,
With no redemption from the fatal tender.
True love will give the loved one to another,
Tho' it should mean the guardian angel given,
Tho' Hell be earned that way, and Heaven the other,
Meanwhile of every joy on earth depriven ;
And more than that, true love is jealous never,
Howe'er misunderstood, contemned, and slighted,
Rejoicing in the loved one's welfare ever,
Tho' to the core the giver's life be blighted ;
    And even tho' their loved one's worth be small,
    'Twill ever be to lovers all in all.

How shall the twentieth century poet please
A captious public, ever harking back
To some old fossil poets for some keys
Of criticism, to hunt him down his track ?
Are not new poets like a patient horse
Drawing a brake of people o'er a moor ?—
When sudden mist obliterates the course,
Each knows the better way by far, be sure :
And so their Pegasus, the public, drive,
Conning old maps—in all than he more wise.
When all have tumbled out and few alive,
And these discomfited, in sorry guise,
     He, lashed and bruised, and tired and flecked
        with foam,
     With perfect ease brings his conveyance home.

Sweet, when thou play'st piano-chords with deft
And easy grace, alike the black and white,
Then my poor heart with ecstasy is reft
To chaos of unutterable delight ;
Thy witch'ries play upon this heart of mine,
Pressing its keys of blackest jealousy,
To marry them at once to strains divine
From all that whitest is and best in me.
I, Memnon-like, when thou, my sun, dost rise,
And thine enchantments wake my torpid song,
Till to thy beauteous charms I melodise,
Thereafter dumb with joy of thee for long,
    Had never been but soulless, songless stone,
    But for the lovelinesses in thy zone.

Lo! as a standing clock is more exact,
Twice in the day, than even Greenwich time,
Those ships have never fortune's chances lacked
Which waited calmly bedded in the slime;
And such as take occasion by the neck,
Before they can have even learned to float,
Will find their first move ended in a check,
And so doth perish many a gallant boat.
And after all, what is the crux of life?
Not to be rich and die at thirty-five,
But to live long, clean-handed in the strife,
A pure straight filler of the national hive.
    There is no gain nor sense in undue haste—
    The best of life comes to the even-paced.

THE best, that is not easy to be seen—
Never until a hundred years have gone,
Removing all the blatant quacks between
The platforms—is the grandest poet known.
Where be the Ramsays, Fergussons, and such
Small spiders that obscured the light of day?—
Gone with the droning, muddy, foolish, Dutch
Poetic humbugs, that ere Burns had sway!
The greatest, and the most worth reading now,
Of our belauded poets lately dead,
Are Matthew Arnold and eccentric Clough,
Who in their lifetime were but little read.
    The ramping, millioned mob, beyond redress,
    Prefer, to Shakespeare's works, a bunch of cress.

Why be like gas with water in the pipes,—
Now dazzling, shortly dark, and nearly out,
An ill-conditioned fruit that never ripes,
A friend, and worse than nothing, time about,
In trouble useless, in good times a bore,
In nothing certain, but uncertainty?
Heaven-bright, or black as Hell's plutonian shore,
No mood to those succeeding gives the key.
It is the luck of few of us to find
Staunch, warm, affectionate friends that vary never,
Who, rich or poor, to us are ever kind,
Would stand by us, although in rags we shiver.
    No treasure-trove will match, till this world end,
    The finding but one single faithful friend.

THE poet's business is with what he sees,
Not with the long-dead ancient Greece and Rome ;
To touch the chords of living human keys
He meets with in the streets, and by his home ;
To be a mirror to the coming ages,
Of loves, and thoughts, and progress in his day—
The imaged illustrations in his pages
From what lie strewn around him on his way.
Above all, he must tell his honest views—
Laying his soul bare to the inner strata—
About his creed, its newer, truer hues
O'er those he stigmatises as errata.
  An honest poet makes men grow far better,
  Ages to come shall write them down his debtor.

HELL broods fire-fingered o'er illicit love,
As vultures brood above the Parsee dead,
When every woman may be treasure-trove
To some good man, and to him truly wed.
What man should have the power to blast the name
Of such a she, with her consent or not,
And hold their helpless offspring up to shame,
That was accomplished ere they could be brought?
Young blood is rash, and does some hasty deed,
Forgetting naught to victims can atone;
But the calm villains who on virgins feed,
Like midnight snails on greens a quarter grown,
    Deserve a ten-times more outrageous hell
    Than all earth's villains, howsoever fell!

AND yet the nation fails!—great God, it fails
To recognise its duty to the child,
For ever setting Parliamentary sails
For grown-up thick-heads, who can kick when riled!
Laws righteous, from the children's point of view,
Would eat the drunken fathers from their skins,
Would have the lazy pounded black and blue,
And save the youthful world from half its sins.
But no, the child is nothing—more is she
The mother; but the brutal father's nod
Sends cloven-footed pens and beasts ajee
With laws that lead us farther still from God.
   The child is father to the man—nay, more,
   He is the king o'er all who lived before!

How like the life of man is to a day !—
Some die upon the rosy flush of morning,
Many drop young, accoutred, by the way,
On life refusing to be further sorning ;
And more die in the swelt'ring midday sun,
Some in the languid, blist'ring afternoon.
Sore gapped the ranks from those clean-spent,
      undone,
When clearer grows the pallid, gibbous moon ;
And those who stumble on to hideous night
At duty's call, God's banner in their hands,
Weary and old, half-blind, yet without light,
Shall surely find reward in fairer lands,
      When in fresh worlds a grander morning breaks,
      And from death's long dark night their tired soul
         wakes.

If we could range our forebears round a hall
To earliest, make them their story tell—
How many a lordly pride would have a fall,
How many a poor man's breast with joy would swell!
Those down would find a long and gallant train
Of kings and queens, and emperors and braves,
Their predecessors; while the great, with pain
Would know their ancestors for clowns and slaves.
For such is life: an accident at birth
Obscures the fine intelligence of race,
Causing of power, and pluck, and grasp a dearth,
To abler human animals gives place.
    This age's serfs will one day wear a crown,
    Its dynasties, like all the rest, go down.

Lo ! as tree-branches nearest to the ground
Hang down their heads, and rarely seem to thrive,
While those high up will nothing e'er confound,
Through their position, very much alive,—
So is it with us, midgets of a day :
The oldest race is ever lowest down ;
High up life's tree, the *nouveau riche* are they
Conterminous with sunshine and the crown.
Yet there is compensation : nothing gains
An undue share of good or ill on earth ;
Joy roosts low down, while woe with weeping rains
Assails high rank, for all that it is worth—
    Wherefore I joy that I am nothing great,
    Nor tangled by the hair to cares of State.

One shall be taken and the other left,
Tho' much the one the other's loss may feel,
Tho' it be parting well-tried blade and heft,
Husband and wife that have been true and leal.
Death takes no count of such ; there is no charm
Of beauty or behaviour in the least
Potential 'gainst his all-unwearied arm :
The young, the old, the fleecer and the fleeced,
The good, the bad, the neutrals in between,
Invertebrates who ever unto either
The seas, the shores, by circumstances lean,
Who, wanting in cohesion, stick to neither :
    Death courses down in time unerringly,
    The swiftest, sweetest, best, and noblest prey.

THE lilac-blooms have found us reconciled,
Entwined we twain shall tread life's dusty ways ;
Our hearts, that were so long estranged, exiled,
Shall nestle each in each like the old days.
Our mental eyes, like those of lately blind,
Whittle the facts of life to actual size,
And now we know the foolish, being kind,
Do thereby quickly grow exceeding wise—
For kindness is the healer of all strife,
The salt that keeps the spirit fresh and sweet,
And, having found the touchstone of this life,
We can watch time cross out life's shortening leet,
   Till after long together happy days
   Death calls us out of life's enchanting maze.

Good, holy Europe has a fit each day
About our acquisitions everywhere,
With sermonisings in the Christian way,
Which means they want to rob us of our share.
If heinous in a strong, imperial race
Like us, to hoist our flag o'er savage lands,
In what way does the action wash its face
Done to the music of the German bands?
To the tame, weakly eats belong the mice,
While the great royal lion kills the moose,
And if they try from it to steal a slice,
It shall be only what the lion choose:
    For God's own law will never be reversed,
    We, strongest, ablest, ever shall be first.

CABBY '92 STRIKES

'HULLO, matey ! strike's a-coming—
    What cheer if't had come afore ?'—
Just my babes and my old woman
    Howling, hungry, on the floor.

Was I ill !—could man be iller ?
    Brokers come, and so did you,
Mates, that never seen a feller
    Beat for want o' pulling through.

Getting better, what a grinding,
    Crawling through the weary day,
Clothes and roof and food a-finding,
    Keeping hunger wolves at bay !

Glad to get it ?—wa'nt I rather !
    Telling missus 'bout the job,
Imps a-trotting round their father,
    Kettle singing on the hob,

Makes a man forget his troubles,
    Vanish toil and care away,
Like the blooming painted bubbles
    Blown by Millais' boy at play !

Two wee pairs of growing tootsies
    Make the hardest pull of all,
Constant finding socks and bootsies
    Nearly drive one to the wall !

'Tain't so bad, but might be wusser,
    On a working chap like me—
Come to that, here's one nonplusser
    I should never like to see :

If one baby's two pink feet 'll
    Hole a weekly pair of shoes,
What on earth would centipedal
    Babies think their little dues !

Bust the strikes and blow the leaders,
    Chasing honest toil away !—
If they were the people's feeders
    I 'd have nothing more to say—

Yes I would, though : give me su'thing
    Where my bread I fairly earn,—
How much more I make than nothing,
    That is purely my concern !

I get more than cripple's wages
    When the master's making hay,
'Cause I don't fly into rages
    When he has a rainy day.

What's to boil the nation's kettle,
    Feed her, without give and take?—
Arbitrate like men, and settle
    This and every blooming strike!

BURNS AND SOUTH-EAST SCOTLAND

The dust of March, o'er hill and down,
Is welcome more than monarch's crown
   In spring's, not winter's, play—

So is the poet's welcome, when
His poems burst on public ken,
   Not when he 's dead or grey.

Pile yet more statues on the head
Of Burns, who died for want of bread,
   Exalt yourselves that way ;

Approve his songs with ape-like whine,
For other nations think them fine,
   Be in the swims that pay !

You never loved them then or now,
More than a string of pearls a sow,
   Or owlet loves the day.

Yet here the truth must be confessed :
They backed him in the peasant west,
   Kind-hearted men will say ;

For if the hard South-East had bred him,
They too had surely read and fed him
    About the judgment day,

Save here and there one kindly souled,
Who hath like the lost Pleiad rolled
    To kinder spheres away.

Pile yet more statues on the head
Of Burns, who died for want of bread,
    Get up your name and bray !

And curse your sires for mean and low,
To treat the dying poet so
    And shame themselves for aye !

Tho' generations yet unborn
Will hold *you* up to biting scorn
    For grosser fools than they,

Because of poets in your gates,
And artists doomed to mean estates,
    Yet kings eternally—

Vile poultry-beaked and tempered beasts,
Whose gods are Burns' Belshazzar feasts,
    Ye cannot say me nay.

DYING

Dying !—a tiny word is this
    To haft upon so huge a fact,
That all our coming claim to bliss
    Is barred to bygone word and act.

While sweet Aurora pushes wide
    The golden portals of the morn,
And sugared joys of summer glide
    Along by autumn yet unshorn ;

While o'er the garden wall there comes
    The sound of voices on the breeze,
With scent of flowers and busy hums
    And murmurings of wandering bees ;

While birds rejoice on laden boughs,
    And all the meadows flame delight,
No single rolling moment shows
    Less lovely pleasures ere its flight—

Dying !—and that before the head
    Has time to bend like ripened grains,
Ere yet the petalled blooms have fled
    And something still of youth remains ;

And yet to die !—to travel on
　Beyond the farthest friendly star,
To leave it all, and fare alone
　To our Creator's judgment bar.

Think twice, you man of anger, ere
　Your lips shall frame the fiery word ;
Think twice, you misers clothed in care,
　Who rob the poor and weak, unhurt ;

And you, so righteous that you hold
　No single soft spot in your heart,
As prim and grim, and grey and cold,
　As any marble work of art !

Think : you will come to this at last—
　You that have taken on yourself
To judge all others in the past,
　Who were as china to your delf.

There is no human worm can prove
　The slightest claim on God above,
Unless our very vileness move
　Our Judge to mercy and to love.

THE SCOTTISH THISTLE

' I turned the weeder-clips aside,
And spared the symbol dear.'

LET other nations flaunt the rose,
And ilka tame thing Nature shows,
We hear with lang, contemptuous whistle,
Thou art our emblem, buirdly Thistle !
How svelte thy pinky bosoms swell
Where honeyed, balmy blisses dwell !—
Bees hug thee, frenzied, each a lover
Wi' heart and soul aflame thegither ;
The goldfinch and the golden wren
Alike thy downy harvest ken,
The chaffinch and the oxeye too,
Dressed in his little hood of blue ;
Songs in thy praise, when they begin it,
A nightingale is every linnet ;
Forget-me-nots far ben thy bield,
And star-eyed cherubs of the field,
Secure in thy protecting love,
Unsullied mirror Heaven above.
Thou art conceived on lordly lines,
With honest, sharp, above-board spines ;
Tho' tempests roar and thunders roll,
And lightning stalks from pole to pole,

Disdaining courtly, cringing ways,
Erect, thou look'st them in the face.
Thy brood thou scatterest on the wind,
That they far other homes shall find ;
Thou dost not keep them by thy side
In fond and foolish mother's pride :
On flinty rock or fat compost,
Where'er thy sturdy braves are tossed,
O'er earth and seas they make their way,
And where they will they come to stay,
Yeasting to larger life the curled,
Effete, unscotch, effeminate world.
Where the sea rocks her dearest land
With mighty foot on cradled strand,
With salt spray washes wild and high
To clearer blue the gentian sky ;
Where storms a grim coronach croon
To lowland pine and highland dune,
Where lie the covenanting braves
By mosses, waters, woods, and waves,
Who boldly, bravely, faced their deaths,
Sons of the modern Nazareths ;
Where maids are kind with countless charms,
Where men are just, yet fierce to arms ;
Where brawny modern Atlas stands
Poising the world on back and hands,
Where freedom won her fiercest tussle—
Fit emblem thou, dear Scottish Thistle !

DIRG

Our fairest roses soonest fade,
Our dearest first in dust are laid,
And leave us mournfully behind
To face remembrance' bitter wind.
Of Heav'n they come : they cannot stay
The grosser touch of earthly clay;
Ever to them the angels call
And beck, to break this earthly thrall,
As fitter for celestial spheres
Than this ignoble vale of tears,
Until they bloom upon the shore
Of Paradise for evermore :
Oh, may we some day surely go
Where our sweet roses ever blow !

M

COR CORDIUM

Too late, too late to win you, sweet,
I hurl my heart beneath your feet—
My darling whom I cannot claim,
My darling whom I may not name!
You cling and nestle deep, and root
Far down my soul with sweetest fruit;
Nor hell nor heaven shall make us part,
Unless by rooting out my heart!
We have endured, like beaten flong,
The hand of Fate so long, so long;—
   And yet the cruel, cruel years
   Bring us not hopes, but only tears,—
   Not till this hell called life is o'er
   Shall you be mine for evermore!

COR CORDIUM

II

In some Elysian golden spheres,
Where I may kiss away your tears
And strain you to my glowing breast,
You, sweetest, fairest, dearest, best!
Through whole eternities I want
No joy but on your breast to pant,
And watch your tender, witching eyes
That robbed the glories from the skies,
That make the planets poor and tame
By stealing from them all their flame ;—
   And yet the cruel, cruel years
   Bring us not hopes, but only tears,—
   Would that this hell called life were o'er
   And you were mine for evermore !

PERHAPS

Ye little maidens, dry your eyes,
　　Your trousseaux get a-going,
Your lace, your lawny mysteries
　　With orange-blossoms flowing.

No longer may you look forlorn,
　　No longer wait in tarriage—
You need not even wait your turn,
　　Here's all you want of marriage.

Oh, no!—it isn't Gretna Green ;
　　We're not so green as gritty—
Wherever verdant can be seen,
　　It isn't down the City !

And there you'll find a famous mart,
　　All handsome men and clever ;
This is the song that thrills their heart :
　　Marriages cheap as ever !

Oh, no!—it isn't Gretna Green,
  Nor is it up in heaven,
Where are—I call it downright mean!—
  No mates in marriage given.

'Tis here—we're giving 'em away,
  Marriages can't be cheaper;
So, dainty maidens, don't delay
  To claim a ring and keeper.

A CITY DITTY

I sit within my restaurant,
   By Lombard Street the place is,
And hark the plates and dishes clang
   And mark the smiling faces;

But hardly can I get begun
   For handsome, rosy Hebes,
That fire men up, more than the one
   They mashed in far-off Thebes!

They 're all so tall and straight and clean,
   Bewitching, fresh, and limber,
They make this poet feel of green
   And rather sappy timber—

As if the proper sort of creed
   Should be the Brigham Youngy,
With dash of Turk in case of need
   When t'other men get tonguey.

This one's so plump, that one's a pet,
  The third's a clinging beauty,
The fourth's a regal Antoinette;
  And if men did their duty,

They'd pop to each upon the spot,
  And get their friends to marry
The three that could not share their lot
  Across the marriage ferry!

How can I dare to ask the fair
  To row them o'er to Hymen,
With every stroke to meet a choir
  Of gaunt, tax-eating Caymen?

Alas! the margin's cut so fine,
  Down to the very, very—
My empty pockets draw the line,
  I look, and long, and tarry!

But you that have the pluck and tin,
  I've told you where the place is;
Hie there at once, you're bound to win
  My fair quartette of graces!

Life's waters changing into wine
   For you will happen hourly,
All think in Hymen's bliss divine
   Of other states but sourly.

For one thing, you'll have gallant boys
   And gracious, queenly daughters,
To split your tympans with their noise
   And confidential chatters !

To love you when you're growing old,
   When comes Che Sara Sara,
When single misers count their gold
   By tearful streams of Mara.

And if this poet's wishes speed
   You, and your wife their mother,
You'll gain earth's crown, a silver head,
   And die entwined together.

MISS KILBY

A window in a quiet street,
　　High up to draw the soft spring air,
With, dressed in blue, a maiden sweet
　　And dainty, standing smiling there,
Her lovely velvet eyes aflame
　　With eagerness, that I should see
Her, set as in a picture-frame,
　　And show'ring kisses down on me.

Oh ! dainty maiden, fair as fair,
　　Till I must leave this earthly shore,
Thine image in my heart I bear
　　Shrined in its deepest, holiest core;
And when I near the golden dome
　　Of heaven, I know there cannot be
An angel there to beck me home
　　So sweetly radiant as thee !

I

Parted for ever, and the long, long years
Shall drive the wedge of mistrust further home
In our divided hearts, till it appears
Our love had never honey in its comb!
Alas! and we will gaze in other eyes
Of dear new loves, though never half so fair—
Some strange resemblance calling forth our sighs,
Some chance remark be more than we can bear;
And we who have been locked in one embrace
Shall be in graves far as the poles apart,
We whose fond arms were wont to interlace,
With lip to lip and passionate heart to heart:
    And yet, and yet, I think, when life is o'er
    Our souls will twine again for evermore.

II

To dwell as dearest lovers o'er again,
Sweet, rosy raptures, soft, delicious sighs,
Uninterrupted by the slightest pain,
Lapt in voluptuous airs of Paradise.
No more cyclones of fierce, tumultuous flow,
And ebb of dire strong passionate tides, when each
Through some dead moon offence of long ago
Surged, moaning, shattered on life's hissing beach ;
No sad-eyed shades, nor yet no shadowy land,
Shall be the bourne we twined may call our own,
But radiant, shining gloriously grand
With all the loveliness in Heaven's zone,
    When to us death, care, age, and pain are dead,
    With life and love for ever in their stead.

WHEN I behold the wondrous firmament,
The booming pulses of the mighty sea,
On God's high embassy all nature bent
With germs of stranger creatures yet to be ;
And mark this rolling world from out her chalice
Spills not one single drop in whirling on,
Firm as a costly jewel-closured valise
Through all the countless ages come and gone—
Then do my fainting human senses reel,
And, like a new-born babe in pitchy night
That reaches for its mother's breast, I feel
Blindly, yet trustingly, towards Thy light :
    Almighty God, we never can atone
    For ev'n Thy smallest kindness—no, not one !

Reproach me not that I was false to thee,
Seeking thy substitute to ease my pains.
In self-defence — Thou wouldst not have me be
Aye weeping, like a dray of brewer's grains!
Wherefore, dear love, I chose one perfect maid
Because she had thy phosphorescent eyes,
Another for her age was thine own date,
Another of thy royal build and size,
And then I straightway settled to despair ;
For each was but a thread in that design
Where Nature made thee fairest of the fair,
And I would give them all to have thee mine !
    If false to thee, I proved the truer true—
    They were thine understudies, the whole crew '

DEATH

'Tis o'er!—the soul has passed away
From empty chrysalis of clay :
Pull down the blinds, for never spark
Of life shall light that house so dark ;
Bring in the pall, ring out the knell,
And while you toll the passing bell,
Bury your dead, and think upon
The time when you too shall be gone.

THE BETROTHAL

Thou, dearest, fairest, noblest one,
   Had I command of all the ores
Beneath the never-setting sun,
   Of all the world's diamond stores,

Of all the lovely stars that sail
   Bright argosies o'er heavenly seas,
All, all—nay, Heaven itself!—would fail
   Without thy love my heart to please.

There are no dames of high degree,
   There are no maidens rich and rare,
Whom knighthood serves on bended knee,
   For whom beside thee I could care.

No carcaneted queen can lure
   My soul from where, with folded wings,
It broods to make thy path secure
   Against the vex of earthly things.

Since thy possession's heaven to me,
   And wanting thee's completest hell,
Be kind as free, give me thy key,
   That I within thy heart may dwell.

So, sweetest, fairest, take my ring,
   Pledge of my deep undying love,
That shall for ever round thee cling
   Through life, and after life, above.

BANK HOLIDAY

The laden trains are bearing far
  The millions from the town,
In many a lonely harbour-bar
  Their boats go up and down ;
All silent is the street, the mart,
  At business no one tarries,
But I stay on with weary heart
  Through longing for thee, Merris !

What are the charms of sea and shore,
  Of gorgeous heather bells,
Beside her charms whom I adore,
  Who all the fair excels ?
I would not lose, if it were mine,
  From thee one single caress,
For all this world thinks divine,
  My sweet own lovely Merris !

The harvest moon is high and clear,
  She'll see, but never tell,
She has through many a thousand year
  Been sweethearting hersel'.

So meet me in the lovers' lane,
   Till dawn the heaven serries—
The very nightingales' refrain
   Is—Come and kiss me, Merris!

Then bless me with thy heaven of charms,
   And be not coy but kind—
Mine is, till thou art in my arms,
   Life's bitter, bitter rind!
With thine enchantments fonder far
   Than hers, beloved of Paris,
Be thou my sweet, my guiding star
   For ever, Angel Merris!

MY LOVE AND I

We two shake hands when meeting,
  If some one else is by,
With just the shyest greeting,
  But welcomes of the eye.

We two shake hands on parting
  With but some smothered sighs,
And with our heads averting,
  We daren't kiss good-byes.

Outside the birds are pairing
  Among the blossom boughs,
And everything is sharing
  Nature's *couleur de rose*.

But if the parting kisses
  Can't be allowed us yet,
We have some lovely blisses
  We never quite forget.

We have an understanding,
  My dear, dear love and I,
That nothing shall be wanting
  In our sweet by-and-by.

And so is all our waiting
  Serene from day to day,
Because with hopes we're freighting,
  To meet at last for aye.

LONGING

I am consumed with fierce desire
    To clasp thee close for ever,
To feel thy heart beat nigher, nigher,
    My own heart sated never;
But longing, longing more and more,
    And fainting for thy kisses—
Come soon, come soon, whom I adore,
    Thou carcanet of blisses!

Though angry fate may frown to-day,
    We shall be one to-morrow,
When once has dawned its glorious ray,
    A long farewell to sorrow:
So fret no longer, sweetheart mine,
    Regard not fate's vagaries,
For ever am I truly thine,
    My sweet, angelic Merris!

DIRGE

When the snaws of life's December
   Drift amang thy raven hair,
Best forget and ne'er remember
   Spring, when life was young and fair,

Nor the roses of thy summer,
   Nor the lilies in between—
What are they to this newcomer
   But a tearful might-have-been?

For the glory has departed,
   For the tender glamour's o'er,
Till thou meet'st thy one true-hearted,
   And be parted never more.

BIRCHINGTON

D id'st thou too sun upon this tongue of land,
A nd hear the ocean roaring far below,
N oting the tiny bays of bathing sand
T orn ever by its restless ebb and flow?
E re Time had laid his heavy hands on thee,
G raving thee with the foresigns of his graves,
R aced not thine eager footsteps to the sea,
O mdurman-like, all battle-crested waves?
S o do I now with pulses full of life,
S o didst thou long ago, and where art thou?
E nthralled no longer by the world's strife,
T ombed yonder lies thy cold, victorious brow:
T he end of greatness, glory, birth, and state
I s dust, thereafter a forgotten date.

SEAFORD

I HEAR the plash of distant waves
   Along the sounding shore,
As each one high and higher laves,
   Then sinks to rise no more.
The birds are calling wildly sweet
   Across the ferny lea,
The butterflies and bees are fleet,
   And lonely is the sea.

But high above the blended noise
   Of wave and bird and bee,
The haunting cadence of thy voice
   Comes ever home to me.
This glorious earth and sea and sky
   Once unto me so dear,
I care not for them now, not I,
   Unless thou too art near !

THE TRYST

TIME, bearing sheaves of lovely things
    For ever in his train,
Shall bring not on his laden wings
    So sweet a tryst again ;
Each minute of the golden hours
    Intensified my pleasure,
Merris, with love's delicious dowers,
    Enraptured me past measure.

We met : round us the nightingales,
    As deep in love as we,
Were flooding all the scented vales
    With heavenly harmony.
The gates of Paradise ajar
    Swung open in the gloaming,
To welcome o'er Heaven's harbour-bar
    The sun tired out with roaming.

The breath of summer in the air,
    The high unclouded moon,
We twined, an undivided pair,
    With love our only tune.

There can't be till the angel world
    At death of this uncovers,
From Eden, like a rose uncurled,
    So fond, so ardent lovers!

What are thy vaunted glories, Time,
    Dead, phosphorescent gleams!
Leaves grey-haired once the summer's prime,
    Or waking day to dreams,
Compared to that delightful bliss
    Upon her panting bosom,
When every fragrant, stolen kiss
    Made her more kind, more lo'esome!

If sun and moon and stars were mine,
    I would forfeit them all,
To be for ever truly thine,
    Thy willing love and thrall!
I crave upon the heavenly shore,
    When death from life me ferries,
Thee for my own for evermore,
    Enchanting, lovely Merris!

FAREWELL.

So long, so long have been the years
    That severed us, belovèd mine,
How can we part except in tears,
    Each evermore the other's shrine?

For only those can truly know
    The deep seas of the heart's despairs,
Who watch the heart's own dearest go,
    Long prayed for, but a short time theirs.

Farewell, farewell!—I will not dim
    The glory of the future days
With aught to cloud the rising rim
    Of hope's serene, untroubled rays!

Farewell! to suffer and be strong,
    While days alone intensify
The thought, that were we parted long,
    Life's noblest boon were but to die!

WELCOME

The vales are fair around me,
    And fairer still the skies,
But where is she who bound me
    In love's delightful ties?
Far other lands behold her
    Beyond the roaring seas—
Until these arms enfold her,
    This heart is ill at ease.

My roses are not rosy,
    Their colour is too cold,
Unless she's by the posy
    To lend her charms untold :
So ever o'er the ocean
    My longing gaze I strain,
With love's intense devotion
    To welcome her again.

Come soon, come soon, my true-love,
    Across the salt sea foam—

Not heaven, wanting you, love,
  Could make me feel at home !
But earth will be a glory
  When you have crossed the main,
To spell the sweet old story,
  And kiss me o'er again !

BRIGHTON

New men shall watch recede the bounding waves
From life to nothingness despairingly ;
As fresher rise and clamber o'er their graves,
They too shall die—so on unceasingly
The individuals, like the waves, are lost,
But the great sea of life and work remains.
However much the single soul be tossed
By wind and tide, the world at large still gains ;
Commotion ever tends to purify,
And the great human, bitter sea of tears—
As loved ones break upon death's beach and die
Ere they have reached the promise of their years,
    Yet sends new generations on to death—
    Is but our life swayed by the moon of faith.

THE TERMINUS

Lo ! as a terminus is rarely named,
Tho' minor stations all along the line
Are marked by day, or be it midnight flamed,
So is it with all former songs of mine
To each departed, dearest, bygone love—
Sweet stations denting all my line of soul,
Each, tombstone-like, requiring names above.
Thou nameless, as befits the final goal,
My songs to thee ring in the dark as gold,
Thy mintage having far enhanced its worth ;
By their sweet burning accents is it told,
Thou art the dearest one to me on earth !
  My longed-for terminus, thy quiet breast
  Give me for final perfect peace and rest !

REST

WHEN weeping nights have come to me,
   And days devoid of light and joy,
When flaunting o'er life's summer sea
   There looms no longer hope's convoy;
When like a drooping rose in June
   This heart hath seen its petals fall,
Nor silver sun nor golden moon
   Can them no more to it recall;

What shall my cherish't times have been
   But those my darling spent with thee,
When mirrored in thy bright eyes' sheen
   The gates of Heav'n appeared to me,
When I from weary grief and care
   Found refuge on thy glowing breast!—
Ah ! never in this world but there
   Have I had perfect peace and rest.

GOLDEN DREAMS

My darling, when the weary day
   Is done, as night begins to reign,
Thou art no longer far away,
   There is no gulf between us twain;
For in my dreams thy gentle voice
   Of summer melts my frozen soul,
And, like a new thing, I rejoice
   In flowers of hope that line my goal—

Nay ! life and death and all their woes,
   Remembered not, have fled away,
And joy and I no more are foes,
   As in the weary waking day;
For thou my heaven comest nigh,
   All Paradise is in thy kiss—
What can I do, but dreaming sigh
   For fear of losing further bliss?

And Fate will not be so unkind,
   I think, as keep us long apart,

o

Whom she so fondly tries to bind
   In sympathies of soul and heart,
But find us twain some Eden yet
   On this and that far distant shore,
Where every earthly care is set
   In rosy bliss for evermore.

REPLY TO INNOMINATA XIV

YOUTH gone, and beauty gone!—Both yet are there
In lasting beauty from thy lovely soul,
The only charm that makes the features fair
And rests the eye, as 'twere dear Heaven our goal.
Why wilt thou trust to roses to impart
An adventitious aid to things divine?—
Give me, dear love, thy faithful glowing heart
To beat in God-made unison with mine!
For who would love the golden morning haze
And fail to prize its soul, the Sun beyond,
Where were all beauty gone without its rays—
Hast thou, dear love, this beauteous lesson conned?
    Soul answers true to soul through fleshly shrouds
    As the sun glads us, whatsoe'er the clouds.

REPLY TO INNOMINATA I

I YEARN and cry to see you once again,
And dread it—parting comes, alas! too soon ;
The transient pleasure, then the long, long pain.
Descent to winter after rosy June—
Nay, as Proserpina looked back in tears
On summer roses, leaving them to dwell
In darkness, so my waning hopes and fears
On leaving you, my rose, make for me hell!
As the dead Flying Dutchman's weary crew
Drive through the wind and rain, past every
    shore,
Peering intensely for one single view
Of that home bay they enter never more,
    So do I wish our trysting-time were near,
    Still more the after parting do I fear!

REPLY TO INNOMINATA II

The day, the hour, the where I saw thee first
I know not, but the feeling was to me
As when on western wings the spring has burst
Within my ken, unsealed the frozen lea,
And in my heart, as in the icy ground,
Sweet flowers arise, busking to loveliness
What relics of the dark days can be found
To rainbow hues, that wept in dire distress!
Now all my thoughts and dreams are filled by thee,
As floods the heaven the sun with light at noon,
To thee sways all my soul, my yet to be,
As yearns the sea to his one love the moon—
    Kissing his chains with joy when in her sight,
    But moaning lonely through the darksome
       night.

FAITH

WE dream not, doubting mortals,
　　Too prone to sigh and fret,
That many glorious portals
　　Of life may front us yet;

That round some corner waiting
　　May be new bands of friends,
Our woes disintegrating
　　With love that never ends;

That e'en our sorest losses
　　Time's mordant may reveal,
Are but removing crosses,
　　Not glories from God's leal;

That in the coming yonder,
　　When we have crossed the bar,
We may get welcome fonder
　　For every earthly jar;

That through the glad hereafter
    There shall be no more tears,
Tho' tears are in the laughter
    Of all our earthly years :

So let us press on gaily
    Till life has run its sands,
And storm, at God's reveillé,
    Our house not made with hands.

SWEETHEART, how near we are, yet far apart,
As if the deep seas roared between us twain—
I down, thou on life's upward platform art !
Will fate e'er let us meet in the same train ?
Alas ! we only see each other's face
In yearning glimpses thro' life's whirling trains,
Transparent by their own impetuous pace
To semblance of rain-battered window-panes.
The train of death may stoop and bear me far,
Or fate may take you further up life's line,
But will not let us dally where we are,
Tho' thou shouldst lose thy lover, I my shrine.
    Sweethearts on never meeting parallels
    Have found in life the fiercest of all hells !

WHEN on the dusky threshold of the night
I muse upon the bygones of the day,
Finding therein no items of delight
Because from me thou art so far away,
Then do I vex the sandglass of the hours
With plaints against my tardy-footed fates,
That will not prompt some ruling, reigning
    powers
To rectify some days from off our dates :
I envy lovers in the long ago,
Who lived within their lovely mistress' arms ;
Our trysts come round so slow, so slow,
With scarcely time to riot in thy charms !
    They had their angels morning, noon, and e'en—
    Thy angel-calls on me are far between !

DREAMS

Had we two wandered hand in hand
   In rosy days of long ago,
Along the dim, enchanted land
   Of love, that lovers only know,
Linked past the power of death to part—
   No stars except thy brilliant eyes,
No watch except thy beating heart,
   Nor sound but of thy soft replies.

There comes to me in golden dreams
   A glamour set in glory, where
We two are by the tinkling streams,
   The voice of song-birds in the air;
Too soon the dainty mirage breaks,
   To vanish ere the rising morn,
My olden sorrow reawakes,
   And I again am left forlorn!

           .

O fickle Fortune! there be those
   Whom thou dost load with sheer delight—
For them no thorn is on the rose
   Of their desires by day or night:

But thou hast not been kind to me
　Through many a long and lonesome year—
Do thou, relenting, set me free,
　And render me my only dear!

MIAOW!

When Burns can sing of mice and mares,
And Cowper glorify his hares,
And others whoop about some rogues
O' funny, fat, good-natured dogs;
And some man says the monkeys swear
Because we 're claiming kinship there,
And women think their mangy pugs
Angels, and kiss their snaily mugs;
While men gae mad about some women
Who, if 'twere kent, could skelp auld Rimmon,
I 'll take what ne'er a poet chooses
Or, if he do, but sore abuses,
A fine, spread-eagle subject—that 's
My clever, artfu', knowing cats!
There 's Torty with the punchy voice,
A very foghorn for a noise,
A thin, bit skirling, tiny tot,
Nae bigger than a dolly-cat!
There 's little Georgie, black and white,
Eating 's his principal delight—
Like pigs, his dearest, darling wish
Is getting four feet in the dish;

His teeth will never go to rust
For want of eating, till he burst;
A sturdy nick, he punches Torty
Not like one cat, but more like forty!
There's Tommy Oldengrave, that flies
From cats and rats, and even mice;
In half a tick he's up a tree,
Not through his fears, but wish to see:
Tho' come my poor defenceless toads,
He pricks them worse than drovers' goads,
Until they squeal for me, blue murders,
To slap the wretch till further orders!
And yet the villain's taking ways,
Ye canna gie him aught but praise;
He loves me, does this best of friskers,
He just climbs up, and combs my whiskers;
All serpent-marked down back and breastie,
The dear, good-natured, canny beastie,—
Tho' how cats come to have such marks,
Seeing the sun has had no larks
With them in jungle reeds for ages,
Is one of Nature's darkest pages.
You cats, oh, why so fond of fish
And hate the water!—how I wish
The past would open like a scroll
And satisfy my hungry soul!
No wonder Egypt worshipped you,
The 'cutest of the beastie crew!

How could they turn you dreadful thievers
Into the best of game retrievers—
You that ne'er dwell upon the lawing
When hunger's in your vitals gnawing,
And each one's just an arrant thief
If there's a smell of game or beef!
With loving glance that never varies,
Tom gloats upon my pet canaries,
And licks his lips, and sighing pants,
Like gallant o'er the maid he wants,
Boxing the compass with his ears,
According to his hopes or fears;
Vice-hunting prudes upon the prowl
Envy his eyes, the four-legged owl.
There's fighty Tom, who'd lick the devil,
Tho' she's no more a Tom than weevil,
But then, 'tis only fighting she-cats
That one can rightly reckon Hecates—
I 'm sure she's just a Joan of Arc
Among the Tommies in the dark!
In looks and ways she's like that coney,
Our old familiar friend the bunny.
There's Tan, a lovely grey and silver,
That makes poor little Mavis ill, for
She grows more lovely every day,
Now that we've given her away—
She'd look at home among a suite
Of Chippendales, and the *élite*!

Old Granny Gip—for sure a witch!—
Her temper's aye at boiling-pitch,
And quiet Tip, her youngest daughter,
Whom Gip, the jade, tries hard to slaughter.
Long Tommie Davis, meek and mild,
That Mavis nurses like a child,
He licks his tail as if 'twere candy
And he a Piccadilly dandy!
Not last, but least, I'll not forget
That coaly demon little Sat,
And one, an old Methusalem cat,
Black, battered like a scarecrow's hat!
He's been, alas, 'tis sadly plain,
A too, too benedicted man—
I think, if I'm a judge of noses,
He must have been great chums with Moses!
Most likely Pharaoh called him Claud,
And that's what makes him look so mad;
Each ear cock up when first he wed,
Like lap-eared bunny's now with dread,
In ribbons o'er his blinkers hings
For a' the world like bits o' whings!
Ye bachelors take heed, for that's
The fate o' married men and cats.
Full many an anxious look he throws
Behind his ears and round his nose,
For fear from out some hole should rip
His latest wife, that plough-nose Gip!

The saints forbid !—they 're not all mine,
The most of them come here to dine,
Then off elsewhere for double rations.
Wee curates of the pussy nations,
I 'm sure you 've only changed your habits,
And that you 're nothing else than rabbits ;
You 've seen the monkeys form the plan
To drop their tails and change to men,
To eat you—till, to spare your tears,
You 've nursed your tails and docked your ears !
You 're little use : beneath your eye
The mice increase and multiply—
I sometimes think you breed them up
As Hindoos keep a cobra shop !
'Tis like your wicked, artful ways
To earn your keep and get some praise.
Oft when I 've heard them scamper by,
I 've seen you wink the other eye ;
And every night you 're known to scratch
To let them hear you 're on the catch.
You 've funny ways, I must allow,
Preferring dicky-birds to chew—
But then, that 's but mistaken zeal,
Learning by that new ways to squeal.
Whene'er you thrum your throat catarrh
Like boiling pot, tho' ten times waur,
No doubt, 'tis hardly orthodox
To be a walking music-box,

But when you screeching mount my roofs,
Like twenty dozen cloven hoofs,
You're imitating in the dark
The heaven mounting daylight lark !
If in your hymns you're far too zealous,
It is because of him you're jealous,
Tho' ne'er a morning lark could trill
With half a midnight cat's goodwill
What man with music in his soul
Can blame a cat's attempts to squall ?—
Some day, perhaps, we'll see you fly
Like lark far up the blue, blue sky,
Singing, and soaring into space,
With all your well-known feline grace !
Town cats are you, 'tis easy seen :
Your opal eyes have naught of green,
Your tails and tempers both are short,
Your paws are hard, and not the sort
To stalk the game with velvet tread
O'er withered leaves and branches dead—
Your very nose is short and straight
And strong, to buttress up the weight
Of brains enlarged with mighty thinking,
That country cats take out in drinking ;
You're brooding o'er the evil day
When, dog-like, you shall taxes pay.
If vivisects or taxers come
To take you from this happy home,

Before we lose you Linds and Pattis,
To grace their Sunday dinner *gâteaux*,
They 'll kiss my bill-hook in the yard!
You 'll come behind and rip them hard,
Until they feel the devil 's come
To bear them to their waiting home!
Poor beasts, I 'll ne'er set you adrift,
Tho' 1 should reach my hindmost shift!—
Like me, you 're born to care and grief;
Nobody asked us, ' by our leave,'
But down we 're dumped upon this planet,
Screeching like some bewildered gannet,
To look for comfort where we can
Between the fire and frying-pan—
And so we 'll fight all foes together
Whatever be our world's weather.

CALVARY

Had we been there, had we been there,
By that Prætorian hall,
To brain the filthy Jewish dogs
Like vermin on a wall !

Full many a Roman sentinel
We 'd cloven to the chin,
The fearful storm without had been
But play to that within.

But it was not to be, alas !
The Christ we could not save,
Though Rome were smashed in fragments, as
The earthquake bursts the wave.

LORD MAYOR'S DAY

THE sun ashine like rosy wine
    Gilt up the spires a trice in,
Through air as fine as breaths of brine.
    With just a wee bit ice in ;
And far away to Surrey Hills,
    Lit o'er wi' glorious glamours,
The rolling valleys, downs and dales,
    More lovely as he clambers.

The laverocks' shrill on Archway Hill,
    The soul of music's censers,
Grew hush'd and still, their merry trill
    Drowned in the roaring answers
Of skirling fifes and doubling drums
    And laughing, dancing drummers,
Vacating villadom and slums
    To swell the crowd of mummers.

As down they came in rich array
    Of fashions late and early,
That put to shame the golden day,
    They shone, they glittered rarely ;

Two, richly dight, loomed on my sight
And beamed on me and nodded—
Both English, of the middle height,
And something barrel-bodied.

One, sandy-haired, with strawy beard
   Split like the tail of swallow,
All ermine geared and courtly aired,
   A ruddy, merry fellow ;
His long-toed shoon, tied up aboon
   His knees, with silver laces,
I heard him croon some olden tune
   That smacked of foreign places.

One, tawny-bearded like the pard,
   Had ruffles round his collar,
They circled from him quite a yard,
   His hat a curly bowler;
And underneath his velvet cloak
   There danced a dumpy dagger,
His airs were those of gentle folk,
   But with a courtier's swagger.

One's een were ever on the ground,
   As he were hunting maukin,
The t'other, looking sharply round
   As keenly quick as falcon.

Sir long-toed shoon at length began,
   In accents deep and low—
They set me thinking of the man
   Who spoke of French at Bow:

' I' faith, God wot, my bonnie Scot,
   We ken ye for a poet—
From the Sir William Wallace lot?
   My name, ye maybe know it;
But have no fear from any here,
   Poets are brothers a', sir—
See, this is William Shakèspeare,
   And I am Geoffrey Chaucer.

' We are allowed to join the crowd
   Upon Lord Mayor's morning,
For any dress may be avowed
   Or any antique sorning,
Just once in each three hundred year,
   As near as may be reckoned—
This is his first appearance here,
   Altho' it makes my second.'

' Indeed,' quoth I, and shook their hands,
   ' I 'm awfu' pleased to see ye:
How div ye like the silent lands—
   I say, and hoo 's a' wi' ye ?

Your friendliness my heart has tirled,
 Wi' love I feel a' tinglish,
For, after Scots, of a' the world
 I 'd sooner far be English !

' Now let 's abroad, for on the road
 As throng as bees new cast-off,
Riding a yaud, to ease his load,
 We 'll maybe meet wi' Falstaff—
Maybe will come, wi' golden thumb
 Your jolly friend the miller,
The abbess prim aye nearing him,
 He edging closer till her !

' E'en to beguile the time the while
 The flags can get a flaffing,
The fun come tell, that bore the bell
 And set your folk a laughing.'
' Sir Humfrey and Sir George essayed
 To tilt in heavy armour,'
Quoth Geoffrey Chaucer, ' each arrayed
 In ribbons from his charmer.

' Sir George was hurled upside down
 Into a water barrel,
And somersaulting like a clown
 In Scotland's gay apparel !

Into a stank of japping sludge
   There sprawled the grand Sir Humfrey,
He swore in good braid lowland Scotch,
   And asked us where he cam' frae !

' And all the court was in a roar
   For weeks and weeks together—
It was a merry, merry splore,
   How they flew hither, thither ! '
Just then the crowd with fearful din
   Bore down on us with laughter,
Swept Shakespeare, Chaucer, far within
   Their midst—I lost them after.

Is ne'er in England heard nor seen
   Such dancing and deray
As gathers in the streets, I ween,
   Upon Lord Mayor's Day ?
The reason why, I cannot tell,
   But so it comes to pass,
Whene'er November fogs are fell,
   John Bull's a Mardi Gras !

Hear forty-six and thirty's prayer
   With voice from out his toes—
Why don't you see the best Lord Mayor
   Running the best of shows ?

So in his tram both maid and dame,
   In furbelows and frills,
In legions came, for standing game,
   Both merry Jacks and Jills.

Then down the hill with right goodwill
   We tear along like Jehu—
What matter tho' there is a spill
   Of girls on top of we who,
Remembering our early days
   When we were over-mothered,
Have no objections to such frays,
   And to be sweetly smothered !

We blink and peep as well's we can
   From out the crowded carful,
For everywhere the works of man
   Are just a perfect marvel.
There's miles and miles of crowded streets
   That look like ending never,
Both Rome and Babylon it beats,
   Tho' they were precious clever !

Of all the wonders she did spy
   In visions, Mother Shipton
Did ne'er see shops so grand and spry
   As our colossal L——

For cheeses big as planet Mars,
  And butter-tubs in trillions,
See bursting throngs their counter bars
  Are waiting turn by millions!

The City's holidayed and trim
  With folks in gay apparel,
All crammed and jammed from brim to rim
  Like herrings in a barrel;
And all the shops are barred and sparred
  With fronts like rabbit-hutches,
That by and by a squeeze too hard
  Will smash and crash like matches.

Now we get out, and push and shout
  To help the fun and frolic,
For here, be sure, are sights about
  That all creation do lick!
Some swagger p'liceman blocks the view,
  Whom some kid apes with laughter—
Just as you rarely see a *q*
  But little *u* comes after!

And here and there some midget man
  Is piloting some lady,
Who's built on such colossal plan
  As makes the whole street shady!

And beefy p'licemen canter by
    With most tremendous dorsus,
That larger looms upon the eye
    Than even their very horses' !

There 's bikers bent like reaping-hook,
    And printers off the plumb,
Because they cannot overlook
    Their extra weight of thumb ;
And many a patient little wife
    With all her brood to carry,
Can still contrive enjoy this life,
    And still grows fat and merry.

There 's plenty starving, sorefoot mikes,
    With two complaints akin,
Their head and stomach both alikes—
    To let, apply within !
And many a stout mechanic lad,
    Who ought to wear the garter,
Is getting clemmed on parish bread
    More sorrowful than Werter.

There 's lads that love the liquor-kegs
    Not wisely but too well,
Are praying for some ocean legs
    And not a prison cell.

Oh for that cherub up aloft
    To steer them safe to cover—
But no, they zigzag fore and aft
    Like hunting pigs in clover!

Some Scots a-kilt are buckling till't
    To show us Tullochgorum,
Their chanters filled, begin to lilt
    Like distant rumbling storm.
Deil black their een says Scots are mean!—
    For fear the pipes get husky,
The pipers clean them aye between
    The tunes wi' borrowed whisky!

But aye the swipes stick in the pipes
    And take an awfu' sucking,
As each one ripes, his mouth he wipes
    And smacks like hens a-clucking!
The public cheer, as whirling veer
    The kilts, their dearest fancies—
To London ears and eyes no peers
    Exist to Highland dances!

But lo! the show is upset clean,
    By what no mortal can see,
And legs and arms and pipes between
    Sprawl like a minnow tansy;

And Scotland stands not where it did,
   Tho' that a sign of grace is,
For only sinners can be said
   To stand in slippery places!

There 's many a chalky City clerk,
   Who looks like fed on pills,
Would welcome for a change of work
   A rise in powder-mills;
And plucky postmen toiling round,
   Like squirrels cramped in cages,
Alas, how seldom are they found
   In more than squirrels' wages!

There 's many a cloud-capt Yankee chap,
   Whose wonder hourly grows
Our blooming country don't tip up
   And punch him on the nose!
Ach, Chermans, Chermans everywhere,
   With little heels that clink,
With blinkers, pipes, long yellow hair,
   And sausages that wink!

And who is this gallant, *parbleu*,
   Shrugging his shoulders there?
Who can it be, who but *Mossoo*,
   With blacking-brushy hair!

For why, ze perfide waiter-mans
　Can not say what's for dinner—
Von veek ahead, it spoil hees plans,
　Ze meeserable sinner !

Hodge, grinning, head spun round and round
　Like pot upon a pivot,
Falls foul of all above the ground
　Till he's as black 's a trivet ;
And when he downs a huge lamp-post,
　It naught excites his fears,
Providing no great sight be lost
　Nor too much off his ears.

Old Granny Hodge, his map-faced pard,
　With Noah's ark umbrella
Gyrating round and hitting hard,
　Does make the whole town bellow.
Pinfeather pups, that winking tease
　The simple country woman,
Are told, they'll do to match the geese
　That browse upon her common.

With crab-like gait, akimbo knees,
　See tarrybreeks a-prancing—
He's more at home upon the seas
　Or fiddle hornpipes dancing !

One hand is hoisting up his slack,
   And one 's far round his Nancy,
Of all his thousand wives—oh, Jack
   His latest, fattest fancy !

Her points are of prize-winning cow
   And hanging Babylon gardens—
She 's free and liberal views enow
   For any ten Hawardens !
There 's volunteers so fighting full,
   They 'll give our foes the palsy—
For don't they often hit a bull
   Even when they miss the bull's eye !

And smug and saintly City men,
   Who look as they had swallowed
A Bible and a hymn-book when
   Their wives to town have followed ;
And loafing, lazy, put-on airs
   Of taxers, vile and rude,
Whose whole intent in life is theirs,
   And not their country's, good !

Sky pilot saints of puncheon make,
   Whose foolscap-folio mouths
Can never get enough to slake
   Their limekiln whisky drouths !

With eagle nose, gorilla grip,
   And hair atrocious sandy,
They 'll keep the Sabbath, rind and pip—
   The world too, if 'twere handy !

With aspect meek and brazen cheek
   And airs of vaults of siller,
The pharisee his head does peek
   Around like caterpillar :
And Heaven has need—it has indeed !—
   Of its own valuation—
He thinks the saints of whom we read
   Should pay him adoration !

And feed-the-poors, whose parrot word
   As for your cash they hanker,
Is, ' Lend it freely to the Lord,
   But lemme be the banker ' !
And brieflesses who ne'er get called
   Save to the whisky bars,
And vivisects who should be mauled
   Till they 're tattooed with scars !

But hark the merry trumpets' blare,
   And mark the smiling faces,
From City bounds they frighten care,
   To Downing Street he races.

Avaunt! ye railway vans and carts,
  Ye cabs and 'busses too,
For once the City's busy marts
  Do not belong to you.

No more in terror of our lives
  We 'll tear in frantic rushes,
With Vitus jumps and cootlike dives
  And most unseemly crushes
Across the streets, all kinds and sorts,
  Thin youths and fat old podgers,
Fair maids and dames of stately ports
  Like perfect devil-dodgers!

But soft, here comes the Mayor's coach—
  Old Solomon the wiver,
In all his glory, ne'er was such
  A swell as Dick the driver.
The sword and mace each window 's out,
  The Mayor 's in the middle,
Just like, the naughty boys will shout,
  The bridge across a fiddle!

The coachman well and wisely thinks,
  God help them o'er the cobbles,
For when his honoured Highness winks
  The craft sore dips and wobbles.

And God forbid that he should sneeze,
   As common mortals may do,
Or flat as Gorgonzola cheese
   Will go our British Cato !

Some lively march, ye fifes and drums,
   With rattling double clangours,
Play up ; the conquering hero comes
   With bigger Zoos than Sangers,
And roaring City bulls and bears,
   And tiny charity brats—
The former fed in Stocks, on Shares,
   The latter, gin and sprats.

Now the procession's nearly fey
   In transcendental glory,
A cross betwixt the first of May
   And cattle-lifting foray.
Oh, let a Mayor's *pas de seul*
   Up Cheapside lead the way,
Like when King David played the fool
   With ancient boom-der-ay !

My heart leaps up when I behold
   Our thrifty Cops in blue,
For each one owns a watch of gold
   Saved from a silver screw.

The marching firemen catch the eyes,
  Proboscis in the air,
Tho' all the fire that we can spy 's
  Their blazing ginger hair !

Ye gallant tars, ye soldiers, come,
  The glory of our nation—
At home, abroad, or on the foam,
  Britannia's salvation.
Cursed be their way till better pay
  Is voted you!—It shall come,
For to the nation's heart each day
  You 're dearer and more welcome.

Four-square shall England ever stand
  With Scotland, Ireland, Wales :
Where is the suicidal hand
  Dare violate our pales ?
'Mid shot and shell and battle's roars
  Come one, come every foe,
To leave their bones upon our shores
  Or back in fragments go.

Fate is to lobster knights unkind,
  They sit their armour raw in,
Bad boys far down their necks behind
  Threw things that wanted clawing ;

And courtiers like bedizened cats
When comes a little shower,
Get like bewildered, drowning rats,
And round them feebly glower.

Although Godiva's fate is worst
And gives her many a turn,
Her breastplate from its moorings burst
And wobbles like a churn ;
And much the maid in fervour prayed
No more miss-haps would happen—
Like Jericho, when music played,
Her under-pins are snapping.

Lord, how misplaced are things in life !
Young folk have teeth and want aye,
Old toothless jades, both man and wife,
Have cash and food in plenty ;
Here, over-gorged, all sweat suffused,
Are hosts of fat beef-eaters,
In Afric, feeling quite ill-used,
Are hosts of starved muskeeters.

Now Billingsgate gives them the slate
In tower of Babel lingoes,
'Tween them the difference isn't great
And those Australian dingoes.

From Thames Street pour the paper trades,
   Free trade them sorely heckles,
Tho' clean their lives as their cream-laids
   And straight as their own deckles.

But how can words describe the rest
   In all its varied courses?—
'Twas like a rainbow at its best,
   All flags and cars and horses.
And all the folks enjoyed the fun,
   Then sauntered home contented,
And many a courting then begun
   Has been in church cemented.

God bless the Mayor and his fags,
   Their pretty babes also,
And all the pompous turtle-bugs
   That round his table go.
And thank God, who gives us anew
   A yearly civic king—
Tho' as for all the good they do,
   That's quite another thing !

Unless it be to let us see
   We men are grown-up babies,
And women too—that's nothing new—
   Are just aurora rabies,

That wilder fling with older wing
　Than when as babies quaffing—
More shows bring, bring. O London's King,
　To make us die a-laughing!

This is the olden version;—now,
　In all good works the foremost,
In smoothing out care's wrinkled brow,
　Lord Mayors are the warmest;
And charities lie flat as flat
　The wealthy City's breast in,
Till bang! they burst that mighty pot
　Lord Mayor's put the yeast in.

God ever bless the Mayoress
　And keep from aught with harm in—
They're always, Matron, Dame, or Miss,
　Kind, witty, sweet, and charming.
Of Britain's huge food-giving span,
　Across all nations feasting
Our hunger-stricken brother man,
　My Lady's aye the keystone.

GANG OF THIEVES

That ill-conditioned gang of nicks,
Devoid of honour, full of tricks,
Who sneaked our locks with skeleton-key
Our trade's own filthy, crawling fleas;
For ever lurking in one's rear
To thieving catch with greedy ear
Some chance remark to profit them :
Devoid of soul, or sense, or shame,
Judas Iscariot at last
Is Heaven'd; for when to Hell they passed,
He shone beside them white as snow—
He looked so grand, they looked so low,
That poor old Satan 's choked with weeping
To think such vermin 's in his keeping !

EPITAPH ON H. M.

Here M——r lies, and be it said,
No abler man is with the dead.
Rugged he was; no heart more kind
E'er beat beneath a smoother rind—
God guard his soul and give him rest,
I'm damned if he's not with the blest !
Know Wilcox, Denny, Pimm, and M——r,
Integrity unto the core,
And there you have at once the key
How mighty England came to be ;
The manhood of clean lives like these
Freshens the race as salt the seas.

ANSWER TO 'DRINK TO ME ONLY'

THE moaning sea but loves the land
That fronts her with disdain,
Repelled, returns with tender cling,
And wooes through deathly pain.

Although the moon and starry skies
Beseech her for their bride,
For glorious heaven she gives not up
Her lowly scorner's side.

So long as this her chosen breathe,
What careth she who dies?
Even so I love but thee alone,
Here and through Paradise.

ON A VERY NEAR RELATION
OF THE AUTHOR'S

He's gone, thank God! Our eyes get sore
To see this weevil never more,
And all his chums, the other beasts,
Are waking him with constant feasts;
For perfect joy he's shunted down
At last among his very own,
And only poor old Satan cries
In piteous case and dams his eyes,
That hell must take this viceful keg,
This —— abortive rotten egg!

SHAKESPEARE'S CASSIUS

He looks as if he had been meldered,
Then, like a herring, badly speldered,
Laid on a board and flatted out
To take the shape of salmon trout,
Or sacking-needle sharp and thin,
Through all folks' business pricking in.
Except old maids, there is a use
For every kind of sour refuse—
Even signpost clergy serve to show
The road to Heav'n they never go,
Remaining through God's goodness ample
A warning, terrible example.
And this thin reptile, who can grade him?—
Only the mighty deil who made him!

EPITAPH ON R. M.

HERE lies the dust of Robert M—— ;
Tho' lately limping somewhat wanly,
His was the sort that drew the bow
At Agincourt upon the foe.
A game old cock, and pluck's own brother,
While one foot wrestled past the other ;
When downed, he fisted up to death,
And grimly fought till his last breath :
Death, badly battered in the fray,
Has ta'en a well-earned holiday.
Tell me not pluck has no reward,
That cowards hold a winning card—
The manly kind who hammer fate
Will get from God a huge rebate.

THE HAMMER OF THE SCOTS

WE grin, as in the words we drink,
And then the other eye we wink ;
How kind to brush aside our rust
And smash yourself to utter dust !
The Scottish anvil little cares
How many hammers out she wears—
Poor fool, to strike on freedom's rock,
And fly in fragments from the shock !
Of all thy glittering pomp and high,
Naught left but this lead boasting lie.
If *we* had only failured shame
To cloud the sunset of our name,
Our soul would rise from hell by night
And melt the record out of sight.

A WOODEN BOARD

GREAT Prince of Darkness, what d' ye say
You badly want to bear away?
'Summat as makes a roaring flame;
Your show is getting beastly tame?'—
Our gentry we can well afford,
But take, oh take the —— Board!

PHARISEES

The god almightys of the trade
   Within the rooms have gathered,
To launch from thence a vile irade
   How others shall be tethered.

As high they cock their Sunday nose,
   Great God a-patronising,
Each entrance-rule unkinder grows
   And steeper hung with iceing.

They think heaven must be where *they* are,
   Those God-forgotten weevils—
God send me, when I cross the bar,
   To hell's far kinder devils !

REPLY TO SYDNEY SMITH

You need it—bring your keenest chisel,
Our heads, not hearts, are hard as Twizel,
Impervious to your pointless wit,
Which is but slaistery mental *spit*—
But as for hearts, yours might be golfed
From star to star, and ne'er get soft !

AN OLD MAID

WHEN Jenny was about to die,
The devil slowly sauntered by ;
Quoth he, ' I 'll take the off-chance here
I 've just got half a day to spare.'
Then Jenny started off to talk,
The hour-hand round the clock did walk,
As out there flew the lies and scandal
Like swinging round a Maxim handle.
Enraged, quoth he, ' By gum, I 'll want her !
Her tongue 's got such an ostrich canter
That Heaven 's the place for such a ranter ! '

Your verses fret my feelings raw
Like rasping of a rusty saw,
Or ritting of a hard slate pencil,
Or gritling of a house utensil.—
God help the fools who urge *thy* crowning,
Whom wiser folk would help in drowning!

What H—— leaves when on the job
Is what they get who go to rob
The trousers from a Highlandman,
Or fat from skinning glass or stone,
But that same fat, F—— his pard,
Would skim twice o'er and sell for lard !

Here lies (he always did) Joe V——.
He tries (I bet) to kid all souls
How much esteemed he was below.
He 's doubly wrong, did he but know ;
He 's not gone up, we 're all agreed,
And serve him right if he 's dee dee'd !

SCOTLAND TO LANGSHANKS

Did you think you'd got me
In a cloven stick?
No, you'll never pot me,
Neither dead nor quick.

Sure 's you poise your finger
O'er quicksilver balls,
Thinking some will linger
When your finger falls,

Bang! I burst asunder
Toils that bar my flight,
Soon as fortune's one door
Clangs upon me tight.

No, you'll never stop me
Dodging in life's offing,
Till you catch and pop me
In a nailed-down coffin.

When you've got me under,
Upon me sitting tight,
Look for fire and thunder
And me at dead of night.

A DYING SINNER

Good God ! who 's this with swarthy phiz
That comes before there 's need for 't ?
The devil sure, it can't be less,
    But no—it 's Doctor —— !

THE SAME

FROM what we 're going to receive.
Lord, kindly send us a reprieve.
Oh, kill or make us quickly well,
For ——'s drugs are worse than hell !

MARY QUEEN OF SCOTS

A LOVELY, perfect, earthly angel,
Whom Heaven itself could only change ill.

TEAR down the cobweb creeds that lie
Full of dead souls along the sky ;
Give us new steps to climb to Heaven,
The old are jagged, worn, uneven.

HERE Fraser lies, Scotticè Frizell,
Who never man nor maid did chisel,
I'll swear the first, but not the last.
Who can the charming fair resist
When she's determined to be kissed,
Et cætera, proves himself a no man,
A pig, an ape, but never human.

ARE you outshone ?   Avoid distress,
Despondent fair one ; you may be
The crimson rose that cannot see
Her own amazing loveliness.

THE POET'S EPITAPH

WHOE'ER thou art, O passer by,
Think of me with a kindly sigh,
'Tis all I ask,—more none can have
Who rest within the quiet grave,
Unless to add a prayer to speed
My soul from thrall of evil deed.

EPITAPH

HERE E —— lies, a little man it
Seems as e'er dwelt upon this planet—
What then ? a diamond 's worth much granite.

Satan for teacher Wood inquires,
And whips him off to mend his fires,
For why, his one prevailing feature
Was Wood by name and wood by nature.

When on the fires this Wood they cast,
Even Satan stood right sore aghast,
The fires went out, the devils too
An awful smoke did them pursue;
Quo' Nick, enraged, 'Let him return,
That d—— old Wood's too green to burn!'

Though nineteen hundred years have gone,
Psalm-singing ages every one,
The world is full of human swine
Who grab the world's dish when they dine,
And get inside, so they have plenty,
If half the human race go scanty.
Through nineteen hundred years of Christ,
Who for the poor was sacrificed,
The rich still use the goads and pricks,
Make true the old barbarian story ;
The meek and lowly get the kicks,
The brazen thieves the cash and glory.

Poor P—— within this grave doth lie,
An upright, gentle soul ; that's why
Friends, foes, and strangers weeping cry,
A man like that should never die.

O Death, shut up ! you're on the shelf,
Here's more a Mower than yourself.

Where is old cheat and never-tire,
Who started for the heavenly choir ?—
So huge a rogue, so prime a liar
Could only gravitate to fire !

Here lies Pontius Quailer,
As crooked as a tailor—
So all his friends say,
But their notion 's a failure.
What ? a mandrake like you
Says each ninth of a man
Never walked upon pins
Since the world began.

I make amends to Pontius Quailer
For likening him unto a tailor,
And not his goose—eh ?—what the deuce,
I 've hurt the feelings of the goose !

BURNS

He saw a sight you cannot see,
The federation of the free ;
He felt a faith you cannot feel,
That Kirk and State shall crouch to heel.
When Witless and his brother, Wit,
In manhood's chair together sit,
When both no more shall be the tool
For greedy kings to play the fool,
When all shall work and none shall wait
To beg for labour at the gate,
When petty tyrants, great and small,
From earth expelled make toast in hell.

HERE lies a mean young muckrake, ——,
One of Dame Nature's window dummies;
His life was spent in grabbing pelf
To waste upon his greedy self.

GREAT Prince of Darkness, what 's the matter
That you should glare as mad 's a hatter?
Some gravid, devil-dodging women
Have tried your temper most uncommon?
You 're sick, Knox Torquemada 's ill?
You come to me his place to fill—
Was ever cruel poet known?
Be off! and seek your hearts of stone
Among the something tax collectors,
Or better yet, School Board inspectors,
Or clergy on the unpaid bench
Who drag folks' hearts out with a wrench.
Poor Prince, I fear your quest is vain;
Our rips have ne'er an ounce of brain.
Watch o'er yourself, great Prince of Rimmon,
Before you Jacksonise the women.
What happens your resistless force
If moveless bases meet its course?

Here lies the soul of Doctor J——,
Whose grave all good men spit and dance on—
I said the soul, I meant it too,
His paunch was all the soul he knew !
Ask me not where his spirit's gone,
You know full well that pigs have none.

Here weevil ——s' carcass lies
For whom no human being cries,
The bug-like thing that was his soul
Is crawling through the dung of hell !

'Tween Kennington and Kensington what is the
    mighty differ?
A serpent is (S) in Kensington, doth make the
    latter stiffer,
And Kennington's a Paradise whose Eves can ne'er
    be evil,
Within their hatches never lies the snake, that is
    (S) the devil.

Though the vile Mrs. Grundy may bridle and leer,
And should serve me a church and morality writ,
To a far hotter climate than this I would see her,
And embrace you with fervour and not care a bit.

EPITAPH ON C. W.

THIS was a noble, manly man,
Built on the Almighty's highest plan ;
He bore aloft through life the banner
Of the Lord Jesus Christ with honour,
'Twas never gripped by braver hand,
Not even in the Apostles' band.
When through the skies the bugle-call
At the last day shall summon all,
Heaven's purest joys are his to quaff,
As General on God's own staff.

In Death's grim terminus old ——
Is waiting for the graveyard shunt;
What does it matter now his soul
Has climbed the highest heavenly goal?
Death may perhaps have booked one greater,
Death never handled yet one straighter.
He also was, though that were ample,
Of all that's best in man a sample.
Reader, 'twere best to mend our ways
To win our great Creator's praise.
Be straight in thought and word and deed,
Be humble, helping those in need;
So when death rings life's curtain high,
That hides from us our Judge's eye,
And all our deeds from youth to age
Are marshalled round us on that stage,
We need not hide our heads for shame
When at the bar they shout our name,
But up the golden stairs of grace
We mount and claim a topmost place.

F. H.

As sheets of paper, soft and thin,
Pressed in a mould outrival tin
In hardness, nay, was never file
Could make its face one bit resile.
That boats and houses, anvils too,
Of such soft stuff are made is true,
So too his active little brains
Compressure is of twenty men's.

COR DULCÈ MERRIS

C ARISSIMA, *my* Merris, in the trends

O f all my songs thou art the core, the shrine,   R

R oses and lilies, wines of rarest blends ;

D elights of kings—nay, all earth counts divine,

U nnumbered by me fade to nameless things ;

L ove in me straining to thee as the one

C or Cordium whereunto my soul clings

E nchanted—of all loves beneath the sun.

M elt earthly glories like new fallen snow,

E ngrained are dust and ashes in their core ;

R egret them not, my sweet, I love thee so,

R ose of love's roses, each day more and more,

I s ne'er an angel here or in the skies

S o sweet as can to me for thee suffice.

Printed by T. and A. CONSTABLE, Printers to Her Majesty
at the Edinburgh University Press